REBEL'S CHOICE

REBEL'S CHOICE

PATRICIA HARRISON EASTON

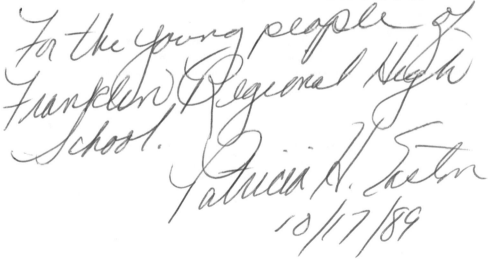

For the young people of Franklin Regional High School.

Patricia H. Easton

10/17/89

GULLIVER BOOKS

HARCOURT BRACE JOVANOVICH, PUBLISHERS

SAN DIEGO   NEW YORK   LONDON

For my father,
who shared with me his love of horses
and
For my mother,
who taught me to love books

145-89

Library of Congress Cataloging-in-Publication Data
Easton, Patricia Harrison.
Rebel's choice / by Patricia Harrison Easton.—1st ed.
p.   cm.
"Gulliver books."
Summary: A teenaged boy struggles to accept the human frailties in
members of his family and in himself when he becomes mixed up with a
bad crowd at the harness track.
ISBN 0-15-200571-4
[1. Harness racing—Fiction.   2. Horse racing—Fiction.
3. Horses—Fiction.]   I. Title.
PZ7.E13157Re   1989
[Fic]—dc19   88-30038

Printed in the United States of America
First edition
A B C D E

THIS BOOK WAS WRITTEN, IN PART, UNDER A 1988 FELLOWSHIP
IN LITERATURE FROM THE PENNSYLVANIA COUNCIL ON THE
ARTS.

For all their support, the author wishes to thank Kendra
Bersamin, her agent; Karen Grove, her editor; Marilyn Hol-
linshead and the writing workshop at Pinocchio Bookstore;
Pier Lee, head librarian, and her staff at Peters Township
Library; and Curby Welch Stillings, program director at The
Meadows.

"Hey, Rob, how about you driving for a while?" Dad said, flexing his shoulder muscles.

"Sure, Dad," Rob answered. He'd been dying to get behind the wheel of the shiny red customized pickup since they'd left Granddad's.

Dad pulled off onto the side of the highway. "I'm starting to nod off. I was out late last night celebrating a win in the ninth," he chuckled. He stepped out of the truck and stood beside it, stretching.

After two hours of traveling, Rob, too, felt the need to stretch. Instead, he sprinted around the side of the truck before Dad could change his mind.

Rob vaulted from the chrome running board onto the sheepskin-covered seat as Dad walked around to the passenger side. He studied the leather-padded dash with its switches and indicators. No doubt about it, Dad had paid a bundle for this truck. "This sure beats the old sedan," Rob said as Dad settled into his seat. Rob turned the key in the ignition and the motor roared to life. He laughed. The ancient Dodge had sputtered and coughed whenever Dad had tried to start her. Rob pulled onto the highway. "This truck is unbelievable, Dad."

"Like I've been telling you, kid, my luck has changed. Wait until you see where we're living."

"You mean you dumped the old trailer, too?" Rob winced, remembering the rusted travel trailer Dad had hauled from one small harness track to another over the past few years. Rob had stayed in that trailer on his weekend visits—lately they'd been much rarer than the "one weekend a month, four weeks in the summer" Dad had been granted at the divorce hearing.

"I've got a 'big-time' stable now. I needed a place with class," Dad said with a grin. "I bought a new double. Of course, I put it down at Tillie's. We Walshes don't stay any-where else when we race at Farmington."

All spring during his phone calls, Dad had been telling Rob about the great stable he had this year, but Dad always talked more luck than he had. Rob should have known that this time it was real. After all those years of racing at second-rate tracks with a third-rate stable, Dad wouldn't have attempted coming back to Farmington without good horses. Only the best harness horses raced at Farmington Park.

Dad reached over and squeezed Rob's shoulder. "Are you happy to be going home, son?"

"Dad, I . . ." The words caught at the back of his throat. Home? Farmington had been home for the first twelve years of Rob's life. For four years now he'd lived with Mom at Grand-dad's, but that wasn't home no matter how much Granddad insisted it was. Home was Farmington, but he'd never been able to talk about it. Not even to Dad—especially when he didn't have a stable good enough to bring "home." "Dad, is that how you think of Farmington? You know, as home? I mean . . . I do. And I thought you did, but I didn't know." It felt good to say it. Rob looked at his father. Dad was sleeping.

Rob focused on the road in front of him. He was headed north toward the New York state line. He guessed they were about halfway to the track. At Granddad's, near Harrisburg, Rob had liked to imagine Farmington as only a short drive away.

He looked again at Dad. Even sleeping, his mouth was turned in that crooked smile that deepened his dimples. Mom used to quip that it was those dimples she'd fallen in love with. Rob had dimples, too, but they were set in a narrow face with high cheekbones like Mom's. Rob's hair, like Dad's, was sandy-colored, but Dad's seemed to be thinning at the temples. Dad had changed in the six months since Rob had seen him. His round face seemed less boyish because of the hollows under his cheekbones and the dark circles under his eyes. He hadn't been that lean at Christmas. It looked as if Dad was working hard to keep his "luck."

Now Dad would have help—not just for the usual four weeks, but for the whole summer . . . maybe longer. "We're going home, Dad," Rob whispered.

The miles passed slowly, with only Dad's soft snores to keep Rob company. After more than an hour of silence, Rob turned on the radio. Willie Nelson's gravelly twang blared from the stereo speakers. Rob lunged for the volume knob.

"Hey, Willie, my man," Dad said, yawning.

"Sorry, Dad," Rob said. "You sure play this thing loud enough."

Dad stretched, laughing. "I like my whiskey straight, my women tall, and my music loud."

"I'll agree on the first two." Rob reached for the knob. "Let's see if we can find some real music."

"Touch that knob and you die. No heavy metal allowed in my truck." Playfully, Dad poked Rob in the shoulder. "How long have I been sleeping?"

"More than an hour. We crossed into New York a long time ago."

Dad looked around. "We're almost at our exit. Do you want me to take over?"

"I'm fine, Dad," answered Rob. How could they be close to Farmington? Nothing looked familiar.

They came to the exit and Rob drove the truck down the ramp. A sign pointed the way to the racetrack. Gradually, Rob began to recognize more of the passing scenery—the lumberyard, the country store, the old stone barn. The memories became sharper the closer he got to the track until finally, when he turned the truck into the entrance of Farmington Park, he found it just as he remembered—the white-fenced ⅝-mile racing oval flanked by the towering, glass-fronted clubhouse and grandstand on one side and the paddock and shed row barns on the other. Purple and white flowers cascaded from window boxes in front of the clubhouse. Dad directed Rob to the horseman's gate, where they stopped at the white clapboard security hut.

A young man in a crisp, navy-blue uniform came to the door carrying a clipboard. "Name?" he called.

"Walsh. Hal Walsh," answered Dad. "This is my son, Rob." As the guard recorded their names, Rob put the truck in gear and started up the hill. The guy didn't know Dad. When Pap—Rob's grandfather—trained and Dad drove, the Walsh Stable had been Farmington's best. Then, they didn't have to stop at the guard gate: they'd just waved and driven through.

As the truck reached the top of the hill, Rob could see Pap's barn on the small rise overlooking the paddock and the track—the only barn with such a view. Year after year, the whole front half of the barn had been given to their stable. Rob slowed and saw the huge red-and-white awning of Walsh Stable on the front of the shed row.

"They gave me the old barn back," Dad said softly, his voice thick.

Rob didn't know what to say, but was sure if he said anything his voice would be husky, too.

A boxy, blue horse van, its loading ramp down, was parked in front of the barn. *Tanner Veterinary Hospital* was lettered in white on the side. "Dad, is Dr. Mary here?"

"Probably not. She usually sends a driver to pick up the Rat."

Before Rob could ask who the Rat was, he heard the loud, unmistakable crack of a horse kicking the side of a barn, followed by a loud, piercing squeal. A huge red horse bounded out of the barn with a lead shank dragging and wrapping around his front legs. With one leap, he landed in the middle of the loading ramp. A second leap brought him into the van, rocking it violently. Rob had never seen anything like it. A lot of horses fought against being loaded onto a van, but he'd never heard of one fighting to get on.

"Rob, stop this damned truck," Dad growled. "Beak, you simple . . ." Rob slammed the brake and Dad hit the ground running. Bewildered, Rob parked the truck and followed.

Before Dad reached the van, a scrawny groom, his T-shirt torn away from one shoulder, stormed out of the barn and up the ramp, a long training whip in his hand. The groom drew back the whip, but before he could lash out, the horse squealed again and, with teeth bared and ears laid flat against his massive head, charged. Rob stopped, his heart pounding. Dad ran up the ramp. As the boy staggered backward, Dad tore the whip from his hand. The horse reared back inside the van. Dad looked as if he were going to use the whip on the kid, but instead, he grabbed the boy by what was left of his dirt-smeared T-shirt and flung him down the ramp. Dad was left holding the tattered rag; the boy, shirtless, landed on his backside in the gravel.

Throwing the whip and rag aside, Dad started slowly up the ramp toward the horse, his hand extended in front of him. "Be careful, Dad," Rob said, but the words came as a whisper. A tall, dark-haired man stepped out from the shelter of the awning to stand beside Rob. Neither spoke as they watched Dad approach the big red horse, now pawing and snorting inside the van. "Easy, boy," Dad soothed. The horse's eyes rolled wildly in his head, but he made no move to charge. Slowly, Dad approached and the horse seemed to settle.

"Do you need any help, Hal?" the man next to Rob asked softly. Dad shook his head. "Thank goodness," whispered the man. "That dirty bugger scares me half to death." Obviously the man was no groom.

Dad neared the horse. Gently taking the lead shank and halter, he backed him into one of the van stalls. It was over. Rob turned to the man beside him looking so out of place in cuffed khaki shorts, white polo shirt, and running shoes.

"You must be Rob," the man said, returning Rob's smile. "I've heard a lot about you. I'm Michael Kail, Mary Tanner's husband."

Rob shook Michael's hand. Dad hadn't told him Dr. Mary had gotten married. Before Rob could say much, Dad came storming out of the van.

"Not so fast, Beak," he shouted at the groom, who was

slinking into the barn. In the excitement, Rob had forgotten all about him. Staring at Dad, Beak shoved his chin forward. His long, narrow nose, which must have given him his name, pointed straight up at Dad.

"You tried to hold him again, didn't you?" Dad roared. When Beak didn't answer, he continued, "I told you the last time: No one can hold Rat once he sees the van. I told you to get some of the boys to stand on both sides of the ramp, then let him go. Not you! Oh, no! You're too tough, aren't you?" Rob could see angry red blotches on Dad's cheeks.

"He damned near killed me this time and I ain't takin' care of him no more. I quit!" Beak glared over his shoulder at Rob. "Maybe you'll have to get your little boy there to groom him. You sure ain't gonna find anyone else around here to do it."

Rob glared right back at Beak. One thing was for certain: Rob would never treat any horse he groomed as badly as he'd just seen Beak treat Rat.

"Quit?" shouted Dad. "You're fired! Get out of here!"

"Someday that dirty red bastard is gonna kill somebody and then you'll be sorry you was so soft on him," Beak said before stomping off around the corner of the barn.

"Well, looks like I'm down a groom again," Dad said, "but that's one I'm happy to be rid of."

"You know, Hal, he just might be right about Rat," Michael said.

"He just might be," Dad replied, "but I can't give up on a horse with as much speed as Rat has. Rat's the fastest three-year-old pacing colt I've ever trained."

"Speed without control doesn't mean much," said a familiar voice behind Rob.

"Dr. Mary," Rob yelled, using the nickname he'd given her when he was a little kid.

Mary Tanner threw her arms around him, kissing his cheek. As he pulled back, she teased, "I thought I'd better get my hugs and kisses in before you showed me you're too old for them."

Rob grinned. She hadn't changed a bit. Her auburn hair, pulled into its familiar braid, still escaped in tiny curls along her wide forehead. And she still wrinkled her freckled nose when she smiled. Dr. Mary was the same age as Dad, thirty-six, but had changed less over the years. "It sure is good to see you," Rob said.

"You, too, Rob. I've missed you."

"The old Rat put on quite a show again," Michael said.

Rob looked into the van at the horse, now standing quietly. Unrelieved by white markings, his sorrel coat flamed. His full forelock and mane were an even more intense, fiery red. Rob had never seen a more magnificent horse. "Is his name really Rat?" he asked.

"No," said Dad, "it's Noble's Stoutheart. He earned his nickname 'the Red Rat.' "

"Well, what's the matter with him? Why is Mary taking him home?" Rob hoped Rat's problem wasn't lameness, Mary's specialty.

"He doesn't need a vet, Rob," said Mary. "What he needs is an equine psychologist."

"I'm afraid Mary's right," Dad said. "After three or four races, he goes nuts. He doesn't race worth a damn until we turn him out for a few days. Then he's fine again for another three or four starts."

"And so on, and so on, and so on . . . ," said Mary, nodding her head for emphasis.

"Before we discovered how to deal with him, he was always

on the steward's list for acting up during a race," Dad continued. "So then we'd have to qualify him before he could race again. Finally we realized that if we turned him out, he was fine. Now when he starts to get unruly on us, we ship him off to Mary's farm."

"It's never a question of making him do what *you* want him to do," said Michael. "It's merely a matter of figuring out how he wants to do it."

Rob looked admiringly at the horse, who had begun to fuss, shaking his head and pawing. "I think he's fantastic," Rob said, not willing to admit that minutes before he had found him frightening.

"I think Rat's telling us he wants to go to the farm," Mary said as she walked to help Dad and Michael fold the wings on the ramp. Together they raised the ramp and locked the door. "At the farm he's a pussycat," she said. "Rat just doesn't like you, Hal, or this stupid racetrack. He wants to live with us. He's not crazy—just discriminating."

As Mary crawled into the driver's seat of the van, Dad playfully tugged on her braid. She wrinkled her nose at him. Rob enjoyed the familiar ease between Dad and Mary. Their friendship went back to childhood, when their parents had been friends.

Michael shook his head, frowning in mock disapproval. "Excuse my wife, Hal. She shows respect to no man."

"There's no excuse for her," laughed Dad. "She's been outrageous her whole life."

"Rob," said Mary, sticking her head out the window, "you're invited to the farm tomorrow for lunch. And I suppose we'll hurt your dad's feelings if we don't invite him, too."

"That's right—you will," said Dad. "One o'clock, all right?"

Mary agreed and the van rolled away from the barn. Dad threw an arm around Rob's shoulders. "With Beak gone, I'm shorthanded. Would you mind grooming three horses?"

"That's fine," answered Rob. And if he did a super job taking care of them, maybe Dad would give him a chance with Rat. Despite there being something fearsome about the sorrel pacer, Rat was the horse Rob wanted.

"Good," said Dad. "That's settled. It's almost feeding time, and my other grooms will be here soon. I'll show you the horses you'll be taking care of and we can get them fed. Then we'll go out for the biggest steak I can find."

Rob smiled. This was the way it was supposed to be—Dad and him and the horses. Not Granddad's way. Not Mom's way. Not that fancy private school they'd sent him to. Not a future working in Granddad's frozen-food business.

He was a Walsh and the Walshes were horsemen. Being with Dad was just as he'd imagined it would be, just as he'd remembered it. And what Mom and Granddad didn't know yet was that he planned to stay.

"Well, come on, Dad. Let's get to work," he said. "I can almost taste that steak."

Rob looked expectantly toward the weather-worn green trailer that stood next to the entrance of Tillie's Trailer Court. Immediately the curtains parted and there appeared the round face, still crowned with fuzzy, pink hair, just as he remembered—the same old Tillie peeking out of her window at everyone who went past. When she saw Rob and Dad, her mouth made a little O of surprise and the curtains swung shut.

"Watch the door of her trailer," said Dad, stopping the truck. "I give her another two seconds. One . . ."

Before Dad could get to "two," Tillie threw open the door, gesturing wildly for them to stop.

Rob jumped out of the cab. "Hey, Tillie! How're you doing?"

"Ernie," she yelled shrilly over her shoulder, "it's Hal's boy. He's home!" Then, turning back to Rob, she shrieked, "May the good Lord have mercy on me! You are some kind of regular young man now, aren't you?" Stepping from the trailer, Tillie opened her arms. Rob gave her a big hug. When she stepped back, her eyes were tear filled. "And to think that you were just a little boy when we last saw you."

"Oh, for heaven's sake, Tillie—he was older than that," mumbled Ernie, hobbling slowly up to the door.

"Hi, Ernie. Is your leg still bothering you?" Rob asked, remembering Ernie's tale of the German bullet that had pierced his thigh during the Battle of the Bulge. It was one of Ernie's favorite World War II stories.

"Terrible, boy," Ernie groaned. "Why, last winter . . ."

"God help us, Ernie, the boy don't want to hear about your aches and pains," snapped Tillie.

"He'll see you two later," Dad said. "We just got back from dinner, and he hasn't even seen my trailer."

Tillie looked slightly miffed. She probably wanted them to come in for a while, or at least to stand and talk.

"Wait until you see your daddy's trailer," Ernie said with a wink. "It's just like downtown around here with that fancy outfit."

Rob and Dad said their good-byes and drove through the concrete park to the farthest corner from the entrance. Dad parked beside a new, wood-sided double trailer, complete with peaked roof and bay window. It was a far cry from the cramped, old travel trailer. It was even nicer than the trailer they had lived in here when Rob was a little kid.

"Well, what do you think?" Dad asked.

"It's nice, Dad," Rob answered, hoping he sounded enthusiastic. Dad was so proud—but after all, it was only a trailer. No. He wasn't like Mom and Granddad. Living with them in that buff brick, professionally decorated monument to good taste was starting to mess up his head, making him forget where he'd come from.

His mother's angry voice from years before echoed in his

mind. "I wasn't raised to spend the rest of my life in seedy trailer parks," she had screamed during one of the many fights he'd overheard before his mother had taken him and left. He had overheard a lot in that trailer. Trying to sound excited, he said, "It's more than nice, Dad—I really like it."

"Look here," Dad said, hopping out of the truck and leading Rob behind the trailer. There Rob saw a small, raised porch with a picnic table and a gas grill. "See, Rob—we've even got a backyard." Only a few straggly pine trees separated the narrow patch of grass from the rear parking lot of a car dealership, but it was more yard than anyone else in the park had.

"Great, Dad," Rob said with effort.

Then Dad showed off the interior of the trailer, furnished in shades of brown with white-and-orange accents. It wouldn't be to Mom's taste, but looked very much like Dad's. Rob liked it.

"I've got three bedrooms. I sleep in the back, but you can choose between the other two," Dad said. "I have to make a phone call, so why don't you go ahead and get settled in?"

Rob was pleased with the room he chose. Its small window looked out on the backyard. The room smelled new, and he felt certain no one had ever slept in the bed or used the chest of drawers, making it seem more his own.

Dad was still on the phone when Rob finished stowing his bags. He could hear Dad arranging to meet someone in the clubhouse. No track had a nicer clubhouse than Farmington. He was glad Mom had reminded him to bring his sportcoat. "Who was that?" he asked when Dad finally hung up.

"Paul Fargus. He owns Rat and that little gray filly you're taking care of. He's got a friend who's looking to get into the horse business. You know, some guy who needs a tax deduction. Anyway, Paul's bringing him to the track tonight to meet me. I told him you just got in and I wanted to spend the evening with you, but he felt I might lose this guy if I put him off."

So *they* weren't going anywhere. Rob forced himself to look unconcerned. It wasn't hard—over the past few years he'd become pretty good at it. "You better go then, Dad. I guess this guy's got big bucks."

Dad looked relieved. "So Paul tells me. I knew you'd understand. I can drop you at the barn. You can watch the races from there and I'll pick you up later."

He didn't want to watch the races alone, not on his first night back. "No. I'll just stay here and unpack, and maybe go see Ernie and Tillie."

As Dad walked toward the bedroom to change, Rob kept telling himself it didn't matter. If he were back at Granddad's, he'd probably be spending the night alone. Mom and Granddad were often out in the evenings. But this was his first night. He could hear his mother scolding, "You expect too much of me—of everyone." Did he? But why couldn't any of them see how much he hated being alone?

"Dad," he called, "I'm going to phone Mom and tell her I arrived safely. All right?"

"Jeez, does she still make you do that?" Dad asked.

Rob lifted the receiver from the cradle and dialed. Granddad answered on the second ring. "Hi, Granddad. Mom said to call and let her know I made it."

"Robbie, I was hoping you'd call," Granddad said. "Your mom's not here. Out with customers. Did you find the little present I stuck in your suitcase?"

"I haven't unpacked yet."

"Well, it's not a present, really. I thought you might need

a little extra cash, so I slipped a couple of fifties into that zippered pouch." Rob could picture Granddad sitting at his leather-topped desk in his oak-paneled study, his silver hair perfectly combed—so confident, so sure, so smug.

"Granddad, I'm working for Dad this summer. I'll be making my own money. You didn't have to do that." But he was always doing it, Rob thought, irritated.

"It's not that much. I only wanted you to have a little extra."

During the pause that followed, Rob knew he should thank his grandfather, that Granddad was expecting him to, but he didn't want to. "Thanks," he finally mumbled.

"Robbie, it's just . . . , well, you're not used to living like that anymore. Your father . . . the track can be such a rough place. Just don't forget where you've come from, son."

Rob wanted to shout, "I'm not your son, and this is where I come from!" Instead, he said sourly, "I know, Granddad."

"Hey, I played golf today with Jeffers and his son. I wish you'd been there. You'll have to get to know the Jeffers boy. He's a nice kid, and someday he'll be taking over his dad's stores. They're one of our biggest customers. When you get back, I'll set up a date with them."

If Rob didn't stop him, Granddad could go on like this forever. "Granddad, I stink at golf."

"No, you don't. You just need to get out on the course more. You . . ."

"Hey, Granddad, Dad's calling me. I have to go. Tell Mom I phoned."

"All right, Robbie. She'll be home late tonight if you want to give her a ring. Call collect, you know."

As Rob hung up the phone, Dad came out of the bedroom in his underwear and crossed the kitchen to the refrigerator.

Dad really was thinner—or maybe he only looked smaller to Rob, who at five feet, eight inches now stood head-to-head with him.

"So you got the old man on the phone instead of your mother," Dad said, grabbing a beer from the refrigerator. "What was the old fart doing—warning you about the evils of life at the racetrack?" Dad snapped the tab from the beer can and whipped it into the trash.

"No," Rob lied. At least Granddad had been there waiting for his call. Dad was staring at him, demanding more. "He worries about me."

Dad downed the beer in three gulps. "Yeah, I've heard him worry before. Next time, you tell him your dad can damn well take care of you." Dad slammed the beer can into the trash and strode back toward the bedrooms.

Dad was right. That was what he should have told Granddad. He probably would have if he hadn't been annoyed at Dad for going out. But he was being a baby. After all, Dad was going out on business. It wasn't as if he wanted to go. Rob could hear Dad singing loudly in the shower.

Rob grabbed a beer from the refrigerator. Dad was still singing as Rob pushed open the back door and walked out onto the porch. He dropped onto a bench of the small, redwood picnic table, and sipped his beer, watching the salesmen from the car dealership showing customers around. He couldn't hear what they were saying. The noises of the trailer park drowned them out—the sounds of children playing, the angry shouts of the couple two trailers down, the TV game show blaring next door. He'd forgotten how noisy trailer parks could be.

The door opened and Dad stepped out. Rob made no move

to hide his beer, wondering if it would flip out his dad the way it had Mom when she'd discovered he'd been sneaking beers from the case in the garage.

"Will you be all right until I get back?" Dad asked, either ignoring the beer or not seeing it. "I won't be late."

"Yeah," Rob answered. "You look sharp, Dad." Dad had always been a smart dresser, but tonight in his navy-blue blazer and lightweight gray pants he looked especially good. *He must really want this guy as an owner*, Rob thought. "Good luck," Rob called, trying to mean it, as Dad strutted to the truck.

He heard Dad drive off, the country music on the radio fading as the truck got farther away. One large gulp finished the beer, but he didn't feel much better. Visiting Ernie and Tillie seemed as promising as anything.

Rob walked through the trailer court toward the entrance. The warm, greasy smell of dinners not long finished hung in the air. A tiny white-and-tan mutt ran from beside a trailer, yapping and pulling at the end of a dirty clothesline. All around him were trailers—new trailers, old trailers, big trailers, small trailers—stretching in row after row, separated only by narrow streets of cracked concrete.

Ernie was sitting on his patio, a strip of grass-colored, indoor-outdoor carpeting under a green-and-yellow awning.

"Hi, Ernie."

"Well, boy. Didn't figure on seeing you so soon. I seen your dad's truck going by and I just supposed you was with him."

"He had to go to the track on business."

"Tillie's off to the races, too. Claims she's got a hot tip in the fifth." Ernie shook his head. "We rent trailer space to a lot of track people—if they was so sure about who was going to win them races, you'd think they'd be cashing in on it themselves and they wouldn't be so short of cash come rent time."

Rob laughed. "So Tillie's still playing the ponies?" Rob asked, calling up a memory of Tillie sitting on this same porch, poring over her race program.

"Money burns a hole in that woman's pocket. If she's got it, she'll bet it. But there's no use in me complaining about it."

Since the trailer court and most of the money they lived on had been left to Tillie by her first husband, Rob could understand why Ernie might be reluctant to complain. "Ernie, didn't you tell me you were going to open up a restaurant in town?"

"Always wanted to run a little bar and restaurant. Serve hot sandwiches, soup, maybe some spaghetti or chili. It would have done real good, too. People are always looking for someplace to go after the races." Ernie had just lost a game of solitaire. He gathered the cards and shuffled them. "Once, I heard about a place that was going up for sale. I was going to go to the bank and see about a loan. I never did get around to it, and it just sort of passed me by. How'd you like to play a few games of gin, boy?"

"Sounds good to me," Rob answered. He had only been about seven years old when Ernie had first taught him to play the game.

The old man dealt the cards and they played, mostly in silence. Cars drove in and out, each one noted by Ernie. A few of the drivers honked their horns and waved. Most drove by without looking. The place was as Rob remembered. Certainly Ernie was the same. Rob had yet to win a hand of cards.

The sun was beginning to set when Ernie looked at his

watch. "Time to turn on the sign. That and getting the mail are my big jobs around here. Would you mind doing it for me?"

"Sure," Rob said, rising.

"The switch is right inside the door, the first one on the left." Ernie held a heavy tumbler out to Rob. "While you're in there, why don't you get me some more bourbon and get yourself a soda pop out of the fridge."

Inside, Rob saw that the trailer was decorated in the same explosion of pink, purple, and white it had always been. The furniture had been changed, or at least moved around, but Tillie's taste was the same. He thought of Mom and how she would laugh at the bright purple shag rug and all the wildly colored, overstuffed furniture crammed into the tiny living room. He poured Ernie a drink and walked over to the refrigerator. It held a couple of cans of root beer, one ginger ale, and several beers. Rob closed the door. He didn't need anything else to drink yet.

Back outside, Rob sat again at the table where Ernie had lighted a small, battery-operated lamp. The dim glow of the lamp and the flashing red-and-yellow glare of the sign announcing TILLIE'S TRAILER COURT—SITES AVAILABLE gave the patio a carnival atmosphere.

Ernie took a long drink of his whiskey and dealt the cards. Rob would rather have talked, but Ernie seemed intent on playing. It was getting boring, but he didn't have many other options. At least playing cards beat going back to the empty trailer.

An hour later, after Ernie had finished off yet another tumbler full of bourbon, Rob began to win a few hands. "Well, you got me again, boy. You're really catchin' on to the game, aren't ya?" Ernie asked.

"I'm not sure it's my skill that's letting me win, Ernie," said Rob.

"Maybe not, but what the hell?" laughed Ernie, holding out the tumbler for Rob. "I'll have another one, anyway."

Rob got Ernie his fourth glass of whiskey and sat back down across from him, hoping the card playing was over. Ernie pushed back his chair, indicating it was. "I wonder where my old woman is? The fifth race was over long ago," Ernie grumbled. "Probably trying to get even. That's what she usually does when her 'hot tips' don't work out." He gave a short laugh and took a drink of whiskey. "Well, boy, it sure is nice to see you again. It's been how many years now?"

"Four," Rob answered, wishing he could find the words to tell Ernie how glad he was to be home.

"As long as that, huh?" Ernie shook his head. "And how's your pretty mama? I always did go for redheads."

"Mom's fine, but she's a blonde." How could Ernie have forgotten Mom?

"Isn't your mother that cute little redhead with the green eyes? About five feet, two inches tall?"

"No. Mom's almost as tall as Dad and she's blonde with blue eyes."

"I must be thinking of someone else, then, but I'm glad your mom's fine, anyway. Since I've already made such a flub of it, I might as well come right out and ask you." Ernie drained his glass. When he spoke, his words were slurred. "What in the hell is your name? Tillie and I argued it all through dinner. She says you're named after your pap and called Bobby. I told her she's crazy. It's something like Tony or Petey—something like that. Right?"

Rob stared at Ernie in disbelief. Ernie and Tillie had always been so much a part of his dreams of this place, of his home, and they didn't even remember his name. "I'm named after Pap," he said bitterly, "but my name's Rob."

"Ha! We were both wrong then," laughed Ernie. "Tillie was close, but I ain't tellin' her."

"Listen," Rob said, standing up. "I've got to go. I promised I'd call my mother tonight."

Ernie nodded. He didn't seem to care one way or the other whether Rob stayed or went. "Okay. Say hello to her for me."

Yeah, Rob thought as he walked away, *even if you don't remember her*. The old phony. He thought of the big scene Ernie and Tillie had made when he'd first come in that evening. Phonies!

Rob threw open the trailer door and let it slam shut behind him. He went straight to the phone and dialed Mom's number. Let Dad pay the bill. What did he care? Two rings. Where was she? Four rings. Where was Granddad? Eight rings. Someone? Please. After twelve rings, he jammed the receiver back into its cradle.

He grabbed another beer from the refrigerator and a bag of pretzels from the counter. He flipped on the television and tried to get involved in the police drama on the screen. Being alone in a trailer didn't feel any different than being alone in Granddad's big, empty house. He got himself another beer. Surely Dad would be home soon.

But Dad wasn't home soon. Four beers later, Rob sank into bed, enveloped in a numbness that finally allowed him to sleep.

Rob opened the door of Tessa's stall. The little gray filly came over and nuzzled his arm before giving him a playful nip. Although this was his first full working day, she seemed to know him. "Cut it out, Tessa," he said, pushing her head away. "I don't put up with nipping." Tessa seemed to look offended and Rob had to smile. He liked her. He liked all the horses Dad had assigned to him: two-year-old Tessa; a three-year-old trotting filly named Meadow Surely; and Sam's Option, his Dad's nine-year-old trotter. Rob checked Tessa's water bucket and, finding it full, moved on to Sam's stall.

"Hey, Rob," Dad called from the office door. "Get Sam ready to jog, but don't take him out until I come back. I won't be long—I just have to pick up something at the tack shop." Rob waved his acknowledgment. He was talking to Dad as little as possible. He had no idea what time Dad had come home the night before, but his red-rimmed eyes and foul mood that morning gave evidence of a late night and probably a few too many drinks. Dad hadn't even bothered to tell him if he'd hooked the new owner.

Rob lowered the red-and-white vinyl harness bag that hung beside Sam's stall. After removing the bag and checking the harness, he grabbed a brush and currycomb from the tack trunk and went into Sam's stall. He fastened the brown gelding in the cross ties and then ran the brush slowly down Sam's neck.

Sam was an old friend. Every time Rob visited, Dad let him take care of the steady trotter who had given Rob his first solo jog. Dad had always said that Sam would be the perfect horse for Rob to drive in his first race. In fact, for years Rob and Dad had planned that he would spend his sixteenth summer with Dad and work on obtaining his provisional driving license. But Dad hadn't mentioned it recently. Why? Could Mom have made Rob's coming conditional on his not getting his license?

Rob's hands began to sweat and his chest felt tight. "Damn," he muttered. These feelings of panic had been happening too often. He forced his attention back to Sam, who stretched his nose forward for the customary pat.

Rob dropped the grooming tools and rubbed Sam's nose near the muzzle where brown blended to black. Good old Sam. Unlike Tessa, he was far too dignified to nuzzle anyone. He was Dad's bread-and-butter horse, not fast enough to be a world-class trotter, but consistent. Dad often said there had been months when he wouldn't have eaten if it hadn't been for Sam's earnings. In nearly three hundred lifetime starts, Sam had only finished out of the money, lower than fifth, fifteen times—a good record for a horse that never trotted a mile faster than 1:59. Rob wrapped both of his arms around

Sam's neck. He'd been hugging Sam's neck since he was tall enough to reach it. He pressed his cheek against the horse, feeling anchored, secure. When he heard footsteps coming toward the stall, he pulled back.

"Come on," Dad called. "Get this old horse ready. I want to watch you drive him."

Rob pushed his way past Dad. "I've been jogging horses for you since I was ten. Don't you think I can handle Sam?" Rob reached for the harness.

"I think you might want to look in that box on the trunk first," Dad said with a grin.

Rob opened the box and pulled out a driving helmet, painted red and white to match Dad's. On the leather band inside, embossed in gold letters, was Rob's name. "Dad, thanks. I . . ." Rob began.

"Wait a minute," said Dad. "There's something else." He pulled a small square box from his pants pocket and handed it to Rob. "A driver needs his own stopwatch."

Rob's hand shook a little as he pulled the stopwatch from the box. The shiny round watch with its leather strap was a driver's watch, all right. He looked at his father, not knowing what to say. Thanks didn't seem enough.

Dad cleared his throat and looked from Rob to the watch, taking it from Rob's hand. "Look here. I better show you how to hold this thing or you'll drop it on the track." He showed Rob how to loop the strap over his fingers while holding the watch in the palm of his hand.

When Dad gave him the watch back, Rob cradled it in his hand, enjoying the coolness of the smooth metal against his palm. He wove the strap through his fingers as Dad had done and then held it up for inspection.

"That's the way," said Dad.

"Dad, this is . . ."

"Come on. Back to work," Dad cut him off. "You get Sam ready. I'll get one of the mares and we'll go a few trips together to practice turning in traffic and timing quarters."

It didn't take long to get Sam ready, and soon Rob was following Dad toward the track. As he trotted Sam out onto the hard-packed dirt, the first rush of excitement ran in goose bumps down Rob's arms.

Farmington's track bustled with the "joggers" making their way around the outside at a leisurely gait, while on the inside the "workers" sped by with a loud clatter of hooves.

Dad turned left to fall in with the joggers and Rob followed. Steady Sam kept an even trot as they did their warm-up laps and Rob, perched on the cart seat, felt giddy in the warm morning air. The helmet fit his head perfectly—much better than the old borrowed jogging helmet he'd used. The curves of the stopwatch seemed to have been designed for his palm.

After they'd completed their warm-up rounds, Dad called, "Rob, pull alongside of me."

Being careful to stay toward the outside, Rob clucked to Sam, who trotted up beside Dad's mare.

"When we get to the bottom of the grandstand, we'll turn. You fall in behind me. Use your watch. We'll do the first half in about 1:10 and come the last in 1:05. That's a slow mile, but you'll get the feel of timing one," Dad instructed.

Rob nodded and waved the training whip in his right hand. He was ready. When they came to the grandstand, a horse was moving up on them rapidly, with two more right behind him. "Slow Sam down and let these guys pass," Dad ordered.

Rob pulled Sam back and the horses went by. "Look at the rail," Dad said. "Remember, you have to watch the traffic coming both ways."

Rob looked and found it clear all the way to the rail. Dad nodded to him and he pulled Sam in a neat half-circle to the rail. This wasn't so tough.

As Dad swung by, he called, "Don't worry about the timing—I'll set the pace. Stay about a half-length behind me." Dad's mare took the rail in front of Sam.

Rob pulled Sam back to a distance of half a length. So far, so good.

As they came to the starting post, Rob squared himself, straightening his back. He positioned the lines over Sam's hips, checking his grip on the handholds and making sure he could read his stopwatch. Dad and his mare began to pick up speed. Flicking the whip in the air and moving his hands forward, Rob urged Sam to follow. He felt Sam take hold of the bit as his trot quickened.

They passed the starting post and Rob pressed his stopwatch. On toward the quarter pole Sam trotted, keeping always a half-length behind the mare. A pacer working faster passed them. Rob felt Sam surge forward to go with the pacer and, though he'd have loved to let Sam go, pulled him back. Rob glanced often at his watch. Twenty-five seconds . . . twenty-eight . . . thirty . . . past the quarter in thirty-six seconds. Sam was so much faster than this.

Rob swallowed his impatience. He was supposed to be getting the feel of this. Pap had been able to tell you how fast a mile he'd driven, down to the second, without looking at his watch.

Past the half-mile mark they went in exactly 1:10. Dad sure could pace a horse. And Rob himself was beginning to feel what a mile in 2:15 felt like—slow. Even Sam leaned into the bit and flicked his tail, the ends of the coarse black hairs stinging Rob's face. They trotted past the three-quarter pole. The watch recorded 1:41.

"Come on around me, Rob," Dad yelled over his shoulder.

"All right," Rob yelled in response. He barely had to pull his right line before Sam shot to the outside. Rob pulled him another foot to the right. Dad wouldn't be too impressed if they hooked his wheel when they flew by. Sam took a stronger hold on the bit and Rob felt the pulling—as if for the first time he and Sam were making contact—from the bit, along the lines, through Rob's arms and shoulders, and down his back, until the rhythms of Sam's pounding hooves were picked up in Rob's legs and backside through the stirrups and the seat of the cart.

They trotted neck and neck with Dad's mare. "Watch this jackass coming toward us in the middle of the track," Dad called. Rob looked ahead. A horse lazily jogged toward them, bearing toward the rail. The only way Rob could avoid a collision was to pull Sam back behind Dad, or to hurry and pass.

Leaning forward in the seat, Rob cracked his driving whip above the gelding's rump and yelled, "Hyuh!" Sam shot around Dad's mare with plenty of time to get back on the rail. "Heads up," he shouted to the oncoming driver, who slumped in his cart seat.

The driver's head snapped back and he jerked on his lines, flicking his whip across the horse's rump. The horse spooked to the outside. As Rob flew by, he recognized the driver as one of Dad's grooms.

"Dusty, you bozo," yelled Dad, "watch where you're going."

Rob laughed aloud as he urged Sam toward the finish line. He could hear Dad's mare picking up speed behind him. He glanced over his shoulder. Sam had a good two-and-a-half lengths on her with the finish line right in front of them. Just like a real driver, with his whip waving in his right hand and his stopwatch in his left, Rob flashed across the finish line.

Sam, veteran of so many races, began pulling himself up without any help from Rob. Rob glanced at his watch. He'd caught the mile in 2:10. They'd trotted the last quarter in twenty-nine seconds.

Dad came beside him. "Well, Speedy, how'd the last quarter suit you?"

"A lot better than the first three."

"Bet you forgot to stop your watch."

"Oh, yeah?" answered Rob, flipping his hand to show Dad the watch.

"You're going to do just fine, son. Just fine."

The goose bumps rushed back to Rob's arms. That's what he wanted to hear.

A gray-haired driver jogged toward them. Rob recognized him as a friend of Pap's. The man's face broke into a smile. "Looks like we've got the Walsh Stable back. Is this the beginning of a new era?"

"I hope so, Pete," answered Dad.

"Sure it is," said Rob.

Six years ago they'd been the best. But the big-money owners pulled out when Pap died, not willing to trust their horses to Dad, since Pap had been the big name. Now, after two years of struggling to stay on at Farmington and then four years of gypsying from one cheap track to the next, the Walsh Stable was back. *And this time*, thought Rob, *we're here to stay.*

"Hey, Robbie baby, sorry about almost crashing into you, man," said Dusty, who was about Rob's age, with the sharp-featured face of a ferret. He flopped down onto the tack trunk. "Had a little too much party last night. I'm kind of wasted today."

Rob continued to sweep in front of his horses' stalls. "Forget it," he said. "We managed to miss each other." A strong smell of beer clung to Dusty. His long brown hair was greasy and uncombed, and his gray, stretched-out T-shirt looked like it had been worn for a week.

"When you hollered, I almost fell off the damned cart."

"I noticed," Rob said, smiling in spite of his irritation at Dusty.

"Why don't you meet me for lunch later in the cafeteria? I'll introduce you around."

"Sorry—Dad and I are going to Mary Tanner's for lunch today."

"Wait until you see the chick she's got working for her this summer," said Dusty. "Talk about a body. This babe will melt your eyeballs."

Rob shook his head, grinning. "Melt your eyeballs?"

"No kidding. She's something else."

Rob tried to imagine Dusty's type. Long, bleached-blonde frizz? Tiny, leopard-print shorts and spiked heels? Falling out of a skin-tight, black tank top?

"Aw, crap," said Dusty. "Here comes your old man. I'm outta here." Dusty scurried around the side of the barn.

Rob hung his broom inside the feed room and then went to meet Dad.

"I just talked to Mr. Barrone, the man I met last night," said Dad. "It looks like we have a new owner."

Rob liked the sound of that "we." "Way to go, Dad."

"Let's go to lunch."

"Let me check my water buckets," said Rob. He hurried first to Tessa's stall. If he and Dad were to be a *we*, Rob wanted to deserve it.

It didn't take Rob long to top off the buckets with fresh water. He joined Dad in the truck, and they took off for the farm. During the short ride, Dad kept up a steady banter, telling Rob how he had wooed and won the new owner. Rob doubted if Mr. Barrone had been as impressed as Dad claimed, but he did sound like an important new owner.

They arrived at the farm and Dad pulled the truck up to the closed Kentucky gate. Reaching out of the window, he tugged on a long chain and the gate slowly swung open. Dad let the truck roll through and then pulled the chain on the other side, shutting the gate behind them.

An asphalt drive led into the valley, ending at the house and barns. The pastures spread over the surrounding hillsides so that the high creosoted fences seemed to make a checkerboard of the whole valley.

"I can't believe this is the same place," Rob said.

"I told you the farm had changed," Dad said. "Remember the old, rutted farm lane?"

Rob also remembered the leaning fence posts and wire fences. The wonderful old barn with its high-roofed haymow was still there, but it had a fresh coat of white paint and the trim had been painted green. White shutters had been added to the redbrick farmhouse and a wing jutted from the back.

"That wing on the house is Michael's studio," said Dad. "That's where he makes furniture and whatever else it is he does."

"He seems like a nice guy," Rob said.

"He's all right. I think I always expected Mary to marry a horseman, or at least someone who could support her. I'm sure he doesn't make too much from his woodworking."

"From the looks of this place, someone has plenty of money."

"Mary's done well for herself," said Dad. All the way down the long lane, Dad pointed out Mary's improvements, the new barn with its operating facilities and lab, the small row of grooms' quarters, the three-sided run-in sheds in the yearling fields.

"Where's Rat, Dad?"

"He'd be in one of the stallion paddocks behind the old barn."

Rob would have to wait to see Rat. As Dad parked in front of the house, Michael Kail stepped out onto the porch. "Hal. Rob. I'm glad you could make it. Mary and Kylie are in the lab reading some blood tests. I promised to signal when you came." Michael pulled the rope to ring the old school bell that hung from the porch ceiling. The bell's rich tone brought back memories of the many visits Rob had made to this farm with his parents and grandparents.

Soon Mary walked up the driveway toward them. Beside her walked a tall girl, and though Rob's eyeballs didn't melt, he was sure this was the girl Dusty had told him about. She was good-looking, all right. Her dark hair hung straight to the middle of her back. And Dusty had been right about her body. But her designer jeans and pale-green cotton shirt didn't look like work clothes. She looked like the kind of girl Rob went to school with. He knew the type too well—they wore only designer clothes, they were always on the honor roll, and they were usually cheerleaders who only dated football players. Here, they probably went crazy over the drivers.

"Rob, this is Kylie Joseph," Mary said as she joined them on the porch. "She's Michael's niece—and my summer assistant. Kylie, this is Rob Walsh, an old friend of mine." Mary tossed a smile at Dad. "Don't judge the son by the father. Rob's a nice guy."

"Kylie and I get along just fine, don't we?" said Dad, giving the crooked grin that deepened his dimples.

Kylie gave a hearty laugh, not like the giggles of the girls from school. "Hi, Mr. Walsh. Hello, Rob." Kylie was as tall as Rob and looked straight into his eyes. Hers were almond-shaped and nearly black. To Rob, they were the most striking thing about her.

"Let's go in," said Mary. "I made your old favorite, Rob— ham barbecues. Do you remember how you used to ask my mom to make them for you? Your mother would get so annoyed, but my mother loved it."

At lunch Rob gobbled barbecues. Much of the lively conversation centered on his antics as a little kid, including the legend that he had once eaten three barbecues when he was only five and then lain down and cried because his stomach hurt. How embarrassing. Still, unlike Ernie and Tillie, Mary had not forgotten him.

When they had all had seconds of Mary's cherry cobbler and Michael stood to pour another round of coffee, Rob asked, "Where's Rat, Mary?"

"As soon as I finish my coffee, we'll go see him," she said.

"I'll show him Rat," Kylie offered, rising.

Rob had been checking out Kylie all through lunch. He jumped to his feet before anyone could think of an objection. He hoped Kylie didn't see Dad wink at him as they left the dining room.

"You like Rat, don't you?" she asked as they walked toward the barn.

"I've only seen him once and he was acting really wild, but there's something about him . . ."

"I know what you mean. I like him, too."

"I'll be getting my fair license this summer, and I don't know how much I'll like him when I have to drive him."

"He behaves himself here, so I've never really seen him act up," she said, apparently unimpressed that he was going to be a driver.

He tried to think of something to say to impress her. Nothing came to mind, so he walked on without talking. She didn't chatter to fill the silence. Maybe she wasn't like those girls from school after all.

They walked behind the old barn to the half-acre stallion paddocks, each separated from the next by eight-foot paths to prevent the stallions from fighting. With stallions, one horse to a paddock was the rule. The horse in the third paddock, gleaming red in the sunlight, had to be Rat.

Kylie went right to the fence and climbed to the top. Rob

hesitated. After having seen Rat in action, he wasn't going to sit on top of a fence where Rat could get to his legs. Putting two fingers to her lips, Kylie gave a piercing whistle.

Rat lifted his head from the grass. Kylie whistled again and Rat bucked, tossing his head. When he landed, he swung into a pace. He looked like a Mack truck bearing down on them.

Kylie jumped off the fence into the paddock. Rob slipped down beside her, but was beginning to wonder how smart she was. He'd been around horses enough to have a good, healthy respect for them, and this huge stallion pacing straight for them had certainly never shown himself to be well-mannered. Horse-crazy girls sometimes did the dumbest things, and here he was right beside her. *She'd better be worth it*, he thought.

But Rat stopped directly in front of them, tossing his head and pawing with one front foot.

"How's the old Rat today?" Kylie asked. The stallion nudged her with his nose as she ran her hand down his head. "Go ahead and pet him," she said. "He's not bad when he's here, really."

"Sure," Rob muttered. "I guess as long as he leaves a few of my fingers, I'll be all right." As Rob reached for the horse's head, Rat took a step backward, snorting.

"Whoa now, boy. Easy. Rob's your friend," soothed Kylie.

That cinched it: Kylie was a horse-crazy girl whose main notions about horses came from reading stories in which gentleness and kindness tame the savage stallion. Garbage! Some horses were just plain rotten. Rob hadn't decided about Rat, but he didn't want to sacrifice his fingers for the knowledge. Calmly, he stood his ground with his hand extended, palm up but ready to pull back if necessary.

"Maybe if you make friends with him here," Kylie said softly, "he'll be easier to handle when you get him back to the track."

Rob had not taken his eyes off the horse. A fly landed on Rat's shoulder and he flinched it off. Rob watched as the muscles under the horse's skin rippled. Kylie again stepped forward to stroke Rat's nose.

He'd been taught that a good horseman had enough sense to use caution around a bad horse. But Kylie looked over her shoulder, urging him to step up beside her. With his hand still extended, he took a step forward. This time Rat let him touch his face, although he blew short puffs of air through his nostrils to let Rob know he hadn't won him yet.

"See, I told you he's not a bad horse," she said.

Rob had a feeling she was trying to impress him as much as he was her. He ran a hand down Rat's neck and combed through the horse's mane with his fingers. The big horse seemed to be relaxing. He no longer merely tolerated the attention. "I think you're right. He sure doesn't seem very ferocious now," Rob said, trying to flash his dimples the way Dad did, although he was never sure if it worked.

Kylie pulled some carrot ends from her pocket. "I grabbed these off the counter when we went out," she said, handing a few to Rob.

Rob held out his hand to take them, brushing his fingers against Kylie's as he did. He watched as she fed the first few carrots to Rat, who eagerly accepted them. He eased his hand next to hers so their fingers touched again. Rat slid his muzzle over onto Rob's palm to eat the carrots.

"He likes you," said Kylie, withdrawing her hand.

"Rob," Dad yelled from the porch, startling the big red horse. Rat gathered his haunches under him and spun wildly away from Kylie and Rob. The horse's massive rump was no more than two feet from them—if he decided to kick, they were in trouble. In an instant, Rob stepped in front of Kylie, pushing her to the side and back against the fence. He ducked his head, pressing his cheek against hers and covered her face with his arm as Rat bolted away, pelting them with dirt. Rat had had no intention of kicking them. Rob had made a fool of himself. He drew back from Kylie, his excuse for holding her gone.

"Sorry. I guess I kind of overreacted," Rob said.

"He wouldn't have kicked us, but thanks anyway," Kylie said, gently.

"There you are," Dad said, coming around the corner of the barn. "We'd better get going. With three horses racing tonight, we'll have to get ready early."

Kylie and Rob followed Dad back to the house. Mary and Michael waited for them on the wide front porch.

"Your dad is always in such a hurry," said Mary. "You come back, Rob, when you can spend more time."

"Thanks, Mary—I will," he answered, hoping he'd be spending a lot of time there.

As the truck rolled out of the lane onto the road, Rob looked out the rear window. He saw Mary and Kylie walking toward the barn.

"You're sitting there smiling like the cat that caught the canary," said Dad. "That Kylie's something to drool over, isn't she?"

"She's . . . nice," answered Rob. But he didn't feel like the cat that caught the canary. That's how he'd felt when he'd made out with Courtney Pierce after the Christmas dance last year. No, he felt a whole lot better than that.

Rob made a short circle with Tessa. The gray filly had raced well that night, finishing third in an eight-horse race. Rob reached under her red-and-white checked blanket and ran a hand over her back. She was still a little damp over the kidneys and needed a few more turns.

The announcer called the horses for the sixth race. Rob could see them leaving their shed row in the paddock below. He felt the same stirring of excitement he did at the start of every race. He stopped to watch the horses parade onto the track. Tessa shoved him with her nose.

"All right, girl," he said, leading her back toward the barn. He knew he'd handled her well. And Dad seemed pleased with him, taking him around to meet the paddock judge and all of his friends.

"Yo, Rob," called Dusty, coming out of the barn. Rob led the filly back toward him. Dusty fell in step beside him and whispered, "There's going to be some serious partying tonight behind Barn Five. Wanna come?" As he spoke, Dusty darted his eyes to the right and left, making sure no one else was listening.

"Thanks anyway," Rob answered, "but Dad and I are going out after the races to get something to eat." Dusty looked disappointed. It had to be some party—Dusty had even changed into a clean T-shirt. This one was printed with tuxedo lapels, a cummerbund, and a red bow tie.

"Like my party shirt?" he asked, sticking his bony chest out.

"You're cool, man," said Rob. "Sorry about the party. Some other time, okay?"

"Well, if you change your mind, you know where we'll be," Dusty said, hurrying off in the direction of Barn Five.

Rob put Tessa in her stall. He whistled as he cleaned her harness. The dark shadows from the night before were gone, and he again felt he had come home. He was still angry with Ernie and Tillie, especially after Tillie had called "Oh, Bobby" when he'd gone to get the mail. But, after all, they weren't real track people, so they didn't matter much.

At the far end of the barn, Frank, Dad's head groom, had finished cleaning the area in front of his horses' stalls. His wife was still cleaning a harness. "Frank," Rob called, "I'll be here to help Dad close up the barn. Why don't you help Jan finish and get out of here at a decent hour?"

"Thanks, Rob," Frank said as he went to help Jan. Rob bagged his harness and checked his horses' water buckets.

By the time he had bandaged Tessa's legs and swept in front of her stall, Jan and Frank were gone. Dad would be up after the seventh race, which would give Rob just enough time to close the barn. He looked in on all the horses and checked the latches on their doors. He made sure that the bikes and carts were lined up under the awning, and he fastened the padlock on the tack room door. He wanted Dad to know that he could depend on him like he did on Frank.

Rob's stomach growled. Neither he nor Dad had felt much like eating dinner after having stuffed themselves at Mary's. But now he was hungry. Dad hadn't said where they were going to eat, but he guessed at the Flame. That was where all the drivers used to go after the races. Rob imagined they still did, and now he was going with them.

When Dad pulled up in front of the barn, Rob was finished with his work and waiting for him. With Dad was a very young blonde woman, definitely an expensive number, preppy right down to her leather loafers.

"Rob," Dad called, walking toward him with the girl in tow. "This is Nicole Barrone. Her father's going to be buying some horses for us." The girl smiled first at Dad and then at Rob. "Nicky, this is my son, Rob." The woman extended her hand and Rob shook it.

"Your father's driving style is very impressive," she said. Rob didn't call a third with Tessa, a fifth with Jan's colt, and a fourth with Frank's mare very impressive, although Dad had been in the money. "He's promised to show me the stable before the others come to meet us," she said, squeezing Dad's arm. Dad's crooked grin spread. His dimples were getting a workout tonight.

"Listen, Rob. Nicole's father and Paul Fargas have asked me out for a drink to talk over some business. Do you think you could ask Frank for a ride home?"

"Frank's already gone," Rob said, not attempting to hide the anger in his voice. "Don't worry about how I'm getting home. Dusty asked me to a party and I'm sure I can get someone to run me back to the trailer afterward."

"Good," said Dad. He fished in the pocket of his khakis and

pulled out two keys. "Listen, this key is for the trailer and this is for room 24 over in Building One of the grooms' quarters. I keep the room fixed up, so if you can't get a ride, you can stay there tonight, all right?"

Rob snatched the keys from his father's hands and headed for Barn Five. "You don't look old enough to have a son that age," purred Nicole as Rob strode away.

"I'm not," laughed Dad. Rob turned around to glare at Dad, but Nicole had taken his arm, propelling him toward the barn. No doubt Dad had plans that would make it more convenient for Rob not to be at the trailer that night. Mr. Barrone would just love that. Good-bye, new owner.

With every step, Rob's anger grew. Barn Five was in the most distant corner of the complex, so by the time he got there, he was burning. Rounding the side of the barn, he could see about twenty kids at the edge of the woods on the opposite side of the creek. The glow from the vapor light on the barn roof cast shadows, making it impossible for him to recognize anyone.

"Rob, over here," yelled Dusty. If Dusty made a remark about his not being with Dad, Rob would leave and maybe punch Dusty in the face before he went. "Glad you came, man. Listen, Old George went to the liquor store for us today, so we're asking everyone to pitch in three bucks for the booze. There's beer, whiskey, and wine."

Rob reached into his pocket and handed three bills to Dusty, who yelled to another kid to take the money. Although Dusty made an attempt to introduce him to everyone, Rob didn't remember any of their names. He hadn't come to meet people. Grabbing a beer, he sat on the bank. Dusty returned with two girls.

"This is my woman Sue Ellen," he said, throwing an arm around a pudgy little blonde with freckles.

"Hi, Rob," Sue Ellen said, smiling and showing a mouthful of braces.

"And this is Lucy. She's a friend of ours," Dusty continued, gesturing toward the other girl, who looked nice enough.

"Hi," Rob mumbled, unable to manage a smile. The girl sat next to him, and Dusty and his girl sat on Rob's other side. Dusty and Sue Ellen were drinking beer. Lucy was sipping on cheap fruit wine. Rob didn't feel much like talking. He barely listened to the others' conversation as he drained his beer. Lucy didn't say much, but Dusty and Sue Ellen talked enough for all of them.

Rob walked over to the ice-filled feed bucket at the edge of the creek to get another beer. As he bent over the bucket, he glimpsed a couple making out a short distance from him. Catching Rob's look, the boy snarled, "What are you staring at, Walsh?"

It was Beak. Rob had heard he was still around. Because of the groom shortage, anyone could find a job. Rob ignored him and returned to sit between Dusty and Lucy. Dusty and Sue Ellen sat with heads close together, giggling. Rob turned to Lucy, who smiled weakly.

"Dusty told me you take care of Meadow Surely. I groom Meadow Mel, her half-brother, for the Donovan Stables," she said.

"Oh, yeah?" Rob responded. "Surely's a nice mare."

"I like Mel, too," she said shyly, looking away.

Now it was Rob's turn to say something about his filly, but he didn't want to. He took a gulp of beer. Lucy looked toward him uncomfortably, but still he found nothing to say. Again she looked away. Her pale skin, pale brown eyes, and muddy blonde hair made her seem so faded. Even her smile only slightly curled the edges of her thin lips. He should try to put her at ease, but he kept thinking of Kylie. He had hoped she would come to the races tonight. Turning from Lucy, he contented himself by sipping his beer. He hadn't come here to look for girls.

Dusty nudged Rob. "Hey, they'll be breaking out the good stuff later," he said, and then held his fingers to his lips pretending to drag on a joint. "We just have to wait until the crowd leaves and all the horses from the ninth are put away. Security's liable to patrol any time until then."

"What if they see us drinking?" Rob asked, not caring whether they did or not.

"No problem. We know the guy who's on tonight. He looks the other way if it's just booze, but let him get one whiff of grass and forget it."

Grass made Rob goofy and he hated that. Beer mellowed him out, took the edge off. He drained the last of the beer from the can. But he didn't really like beer, either—at least not the taste. He hurled the empty can into the woods, feeling some satisfaction when it crashed against a tree trunk. Lucy got up, mumbling something about getting another glass of wine.

She didn't return. When Rob went to get another beer, he saw her talking with some other guy. He was relieved. He wasn't up to being social. All he wanted was to drink enough, and maybe smoke enough, to blunt his anger.

"Hi," cooed the girl lounging by the tub of beer. Rob recognized her as the girl who had been with Beak, but Beak wasn't around now.

Rob gave her a halfhearted wave and reached for a beer. The girl rose and helped herself to a can, almost losing her balance as she bent over. Rob started back to where he'd been sitting.

"Don't run off so fast," called the girl, trying to catch up to him. "You're too cute to be sitting all alone." She took his arm. He could feel her breast, naked under the thin halter top, as she pressed against him. Rob looked at her. She could have been any age from nineteen to thirty. A great mane of strawlike blonde hair tumbled from her head. Some of it looped in front of her right eye, but she didn't seem to notice. Her smile revealed a chipped front tooth. Rob ran his eyes over her body—those full breasts and long legs.

"Come on," Rob said. "I'm sitting over here." Not sure if he led her or she pushed him, they arrived back at the spot where he'd been sitting. Rob plopped onto the grass. The girl, who already had mud stains on the back of her tight pink shorts, fell onto the bank into what Rob knew was a wet spot. She stretched out her long, dirt-streaked legs and wiggled her muddy bare feet. Inching closer to Rob, she leaned back on her elbows so that her breasts strained against the tight purple top. Maybe she could do for him what the beer still hadn't.

"So you're Hal Walsh's son?" she asked. Before Rob could answer, she continued, "I'd love to get a job grooming with your stable instead of that gypsy outfit I'm with. Your dad's something else. What a hunk." Rob was beginning to dislike her. "My name's Dixie," she said, rolling over on her side and running a hand through his hair. She smelled strongly of sweat, horses, and beer. She snuggled closer. So she thought Dad was a hunk, huh? Nicole had seemed to think so, too, and by now Dad was probably pressing his knee against hers in whatever bar they'd gone to. The anger began to rise. Dixie slipped her arms around his neck, pulling him over onto her. He pressed his lips into hers—hard.

Suddenly hands had him by his shirt collar, pulling him away from Dixie. Rob whirled, leaping to his feet, and found himself staring into Beak's bloodshot eyes.

"That's mine tonight, Walsh," Beak snarled, gesturing toward Dixie who lay back in the grass staring stupidly at them. "Go on home to daddy, little boy. You're out of your league." Beak drew back his fist, but before he could throw a punch, Rob smashed into him, fists flailing. Again and again he slammed into Beak's stomach, his ribs, his face. Beak was either very drunk or very slow, because he never landed a punch. Rob could hear voices yelling for him to stop, but he kept on punching. Someone grabbed his arm as he pulled back for another blow. Beak began to sway, blood running from his nose, his eyes shut.

"Rob, no!" Dusty yelled, restraining his arm. Rob took a breath and looked around, his glance passing over Dusty to where Dixie still lay on the grass. She looked frightened— almost terrified. All around him shocked faces stared. Rob jerked his arm loose. God, what was he doing? He shoved his way past Beak, knocking him finally to the ground.

He stepped over Beak to get to the tub of beer cans. Before stomping off, he grabbed three more beers. No one tried to stop him. They moved out of his way to let him pass.

Reaching into his pocket, he felt the keys to the room. Building One had to be somewhere near their barn. He started off in that direction. Only the glow of the vapor lamps at each end of the barns gave light to the darkened shed rows. He sipped on a beer as he wandered, turning between two barns and searching for his building. The anger was gone, but the sadness that replaced it pulled painfully at the back of his throat. He wasn't going to cry. He'd promised himself that a long time ago—no more tears.

He passed Buildings Four and Seven, but not Five and Six. This place was a maze. He drained his beer. To hell with Building One. He was never going to find it anyway. He turned right, hoping he was heading toward his barn. He wasn't, but after emerging from between two shed rows, he spotted the administration building. From there he had no trouble finding the barn.

Without turning on the lights, he flopped on a bale of hay in the feed room. His heart pounded. He ripped the tab off the last can of beer and downed it as quickly as he could, hoping it would keep away the feelings of panic. Still he wasn't drowsy. Finally, he curled up on a pile of loose straw. Trembling and bathed in sweat, he waited for sleep to come.

6

The next morning, Dusty was full of talk about how Rob had beaten the hell out of Beak, exclaiming "Wow, man, you should have seen it!" to anyone who would listen. Dad was full of talk about the buying trip he was going on with Mr. Barrone. Rob wished they all wouldn't talk so loudly. He felt awful. Three beers always made him a little fuzzy the morning after, but six beers wrecked him. Belching, he dragged the manure basket out of Tessa's stall, nearly bumping into Dad.

"Looks like you had a rough night," Dad said. Rob gave him a sour look. "Put down that basket and come here. I want to talk to you." *Here comes the lecture*, Rob thought. He really wasn't up to it. Dad sat down on Tessa's tack trunk and Rob reluctantly joined him. "I overheard Dusty telling Frank and Jan about your fight last night. Boy, would I have loved to see you tear into that little weasel. But are you okay?"

"Don't worry about it," Rob snapped.

"Well, I don't see any bruises. I'm sure Beak didn't get any more than he deserved, but you'd better watch out for him. He is one mean little bastard."

"Don't you worry about me. I told you—I can take care of myself," Rob answered harshly.

"Look, I wouldn't be going on this trip if I didn't know that. I just want you to be careful. I used to sneak a few drinks myself when I was your age. Around a racetrack you have to be careful who you drink with. Do you understand? There's a group at this track that's not too savory."

Rob glared at Dad. Mom sure wouldn't feel this way about his fighting and drinking. "I can take care of myself," he repeated.

"I know you can. I'm depending on you while I'm away. Frank is officially in charge because he knows how the stable is run, but you've got to keep an eye on things for me, okay? I told Frank I'd leave you a phone number so you could get in touch with me if necessary."

Rob nodded curtly. This was like when he was twelve and Granddad went away on business, telling him to be the man and take care of his mommy. Bull crap!

"What's the matter?" asked Dad.

"Nothing."

Dad turned to walk back down the shed row. "Let's go out for lunch. I'll be ready in about an hour," he called over his shoulder.

"I can't—Mary's taking me to the farm this afternoon." Dad looked back at Rob. Did Dad expect him to change his plans? Well, he wasn't going to. This morning in the cafeteria Mary and Kylie had asked him to the farm, and he was going.

"Well . . . all right," Dad said. "Do you need me to pick you up later?"

"Mary said she had to come back to the track late today

and she'd give me a ride." He didn't need Dad—maybe not at all. There were plenty of kids his age on their own at the racetrack. A groom's wages could support him pretty well if he lived in the grooms' quarters and ate in the track kitchen.

"I'd let you take the truck, but what with going away and all I have errands to run."

"I told you. I have a ride."

"How about dinner then?"

"I don't know," Rob answered, determined not to go soft. But Dad looked hurt. "Sure, I'd like to go to dinner."

"Good. It'll have to be early. We have two horses racing tonight. Pick you up here at five."

Rob nodded and Dad left. Rob threw himself into his work, managing to finish early. Frank pointed out the way to Building One, across the road and one barn over. Hoping Dad kept a change of clothes there, Rob went to find it. He had little trouble this time finding the single-story, concrete-block building.

The door to room 24 swung open to reveal a tiny cubicle no more than seven feet wide and nine feet long—enough space for a cot, a nightstand, and a small dresser. Several shirts hung from one of the hooks on the wall. Since Dad and he were the same size, any of them would do.

Rob chose a kelly-green knit shirt. Mom always said he looked good in green because of his hazel eyes. Rob checked the drawers of the dresser. Good, Dad had provided soap and a towel. A shower would help.

Later, squeezed into the cab of Mary's truck next to Kylie, he was glad of the change of shirts and the shower and the peppermint gum he chewed to rid his mouth of the beer fuzzies. Although the shower had helped him perk up, the sight of Kylie had done so even more.

But he couldn't be alone with her until after lunch, when they went to see Rat. On the way to the stallion paddocks, Rob groped for something clever to say. He never had been smooth with girls. An orange barn cat darted in front of them, followed by two orange-and-white striped kittens. Kylie scooped up one of the kittens and rubbed it under her chin. He sure didn't want to blow it with her.

"I'm really glad you came this afternoon," she said with a comfortable smile, releasing the kitten, who scampered after its mother.

"I'm glad I did, too. I want to see if I can win the old Rat over before he comes back to the track on Tuesday," Rob said. Now she'd think he'd come just to see the horse. "You'll help me, won't you? After all, it was your idea." That was so sappy even *he* wanted to puke.

"Sure," she said, pulling some carrot pieces from her jeans pocket. "I'm very good at smuggling carrots out of the kitchen."

They neared the paddock and Rob could see Rat running along the upper fence line. Climbing the fence, Kylie whistled. Just as he had the day before, Rat came charging toward them. This time Rob didn't hesitate to step into the paddock beside Kylie. Rat came to a prancing stop right in front of them.

Kylie slipped Rob some carrot ends. "Go ahead. You give him something first."

Rob held out his hand, the carrots resting on his palm. The horse took them without hesitation.

"He remembers you from yesterday," said Kylie.

"Maybe he does." He took another carrot end from Kylie and fed it to Rat, enjoying the touch of the soft, warm muzzle.

Kylie also began to feed the carrot ends to Rat. Soon they

were gone. Rob expected Rat to give him a nip of protest. Rat only pushed his nose into their hands searching for more carrots.

"Let's take him into the barn and brush him." Without waiting for his answer, she started over the fence. "I'll get a lead shank."

Rob was left alone with Rat. Some of his silky red mane was stuck under his halter. As Rob reached up to free it, he looked into the horse's eye. Old horsemen claimed you could tell a lot about a horse by the kind of "eye" he had. Rat definitely didn't have a quiet and steady eye like Sam had. Rat nipped at Rob's arm. He hadn't been too serious about it or he would have connected.

Kylie came out of the barn with the lead shank. Rob, taking the side of Rat's halter, led him over to the gate.

Inside the barn Rat surprised him by backing quietly into the cross ties in the cement-floored grooming area. Kylie tossed Rob a currycomb and brush and then grabbed one of each for herself. "You take the right side and I'll take the left," she said.

Rob began to rub in a circle with the currycomb. Rat must have been rolling, because little puffs of dust shot out from under Rob's hand. The brush whisked away the remaining dust, and then Rob ran his hands over Rat's neck. Rat stood still, actually seeming to enjoy the attention. Rob repeated the procedure on Rat's back and shoulder.

"I've seen grooms running their hands over horses like that before. What's it supposed to do?"

"The oil from your hands makes their coats shine. Try it."

Kylie ran her hands down Rat's neck several times. "It does. Mary told me you know a lot about horses."

"I've been around them all my life. Not that much since

Mom and Dad divorced, but every time I visit Dad he gives me a couple to take care of."

"This is all new to me. Sometimes I have no idea what I'm doing or why. I mean, Mary's always there to help, but it's so frustrating," she said, rubbing her hands over Rat's back.

Rob brought his hands up to stroke Rat's back. "You do all right," he said, smiling at her.

"I don't know. It really worries me. The competition for vet school is unbelievable. If you don't have summers working with a vet, forget it. Good grades aren't enough. But then, if I'm no good at it, why am I doing it?"

Rob looked at Kylie, who had stopped brushing Rat and had a look of intensity on her face Rob didn't like. "Don't you think you're taking all this a little bit too seriously? I mean, what are you going to be next year, a junior?"

"No, a sophomore. But that's just it. I'm not really sure I want to be a vet. Most of my friends already know where they want to go to college and what they're going to major in."

"Jeez, and you've only got three more years to decide," Rob sneered. "I'll bet you make straight A's, don't you?"

Kylie blushed and went back to brushing Rat. "Grades are important. There are a lot of kids out there with good grades plus connections. All I have is good grades, so they have to be the best."

She was a "cutthroat." The school he went to was full of them. To a cutthroat, good grades came before anything, and a cutthroat would do anything to get them, including sucking up to teachers. Rob went on brushing Rat.

"Don't tell me you don't worry about college. You're going to be a junior. All the juniors I know are obsessed with grades and figuring out what college they can get into."

"Not all of us. Some of us may not even go to college." And

if he had to go, Mom had let him know that it was taken care of. Granddad had already spoken to the admissions office of the small liberal arts college that was his alma mater, where he served as a trustee. All Rob had to do was not go below a C average. That would probably irritate Kylie as much as it did him.

"I'm sorry, Rob. Mom, Michael, *everybody* tells me I'm too worked up about this," Kylie said. "Really, I know everyone doesn't have to go to college."

Rob didn't answer. He squatted to run the brush down Rat's front leg.

"I mean," Kylie continued, "I'm sure you have plans to do something . . .?"

"The Walshes have been horsemen for three generations. I was thinking about going into the business with Dad." Rob stood, watching for her reaction.

Kylie looked surprised. She knelt to brush Rat's legs. "Is that really what you want to do?" she asked.

"What's wrong with it?" She probably thought she was too good for a driver. Like Granddad and Mom, she must think being a horseman just wasn't good enough.

"Nothing's wrong with it." Kylie stood and leaned against the wall, studying him. "So many people at the track . . . I'm sorry. I talk too much."

"No. Finish what you were going to say." He'd find out what she was like right now.

"Look. I don't mean you or your dad when I say this. A lot of people at the track seem to have their lives together, but so many of them don't know anything but horses. Some of them don't ever even go to a movie, for Pete's sake, or play a game of tennis, or read a book. It's like they've put their lives on the track and all they do is chase themselves around in circles."

"So what? Do you really believe that other people live better?"

"I don't know. But the world seems too big to cut yourself off, to only live in one small part of it." Her dark eyes stared straight into his, self-righteous and challenging.

Rob looked away. No one had the right to tell him how to live. "Well, I'm sorry to disappoint you, but if my only choices are to stay here at the track or go home to my mother, the real-estate queen, and end up working in that frozen-food factory with her old man, I think I'll stay here." Rob hurled his currycomb onto the shelf, where it landed with a thud. Rat gathered his haunches under him to bolt. Kylie and Rob both darted to the front of the horse, grabbing the chains and trying to calm him. "Easy, fella," soothed Rob.

"Whoa, boy," said Kylie, stroking Rat's neck. Before he settled, the big horse gave one final kick of protest that resounded off the back wall. She shook her head, looking amused. "Frankly, I don't know which of you is more temperamental."

"Sorry. It's a sore subject."

"No, Rob—I'm sorry. I didn't have any right to question you." Kylie reached out and laid her hand on his arm.

Rob didn't want to question her, either. Maybe she wasn't a grade-grubbing snob. Even if she was, he didn't care. He covered her hand with his and gave it a squeeze.

She reached into her hip pocket and pulled out a metal comb, which she thrust at him. "Here, you do his mane," she said. "I'll take his tail."

Rob reached between Rat's ears to comb his forelock. Pinning his ears, Rat dove at him, barely missing his extended forearm. Rob jumped into the aisle.

"I forgot to tell you, he hates to have his forelock combed," said Kylie, trying not to laugh.

"Jeez. I can tell you right now—he's more temperamental than I am." Rob moved carefully to Rat's side and cautiously began to comb his mane.

When they had Rat shining to their satisfaction, Rob, with Kylie walking beside him, led Rat back to his paddock. Even when the horse walked slowly, there was a spring to his step. If Rob could just learn what bothered Rat and what didn't, he'd be able to get along with him back at the track. He unsnapped the lead shank, releasing Rat into the paddock. Once he knew he was free, the horse tossed his head and kicked up his heels before running off to the far corner of his field.

"He is gorgeous," Kylie sighed. "Mary says if he could learn to behave and channel all that energy into speed, he'd probably be one of the world's fastest pacers."

Rob watched the horse, who now paced toward them. He liked Rat just the way he was and felt certain he'd be able to handle him. He could even picture himself driving the powerful red horse. He glanced at Kylie and found her looking at him.

The porch bell began to clang. Rob checked his watch. It was time for Mary to take him back to the track.

"Race you to the truck," Kylie called, already running.

"Cheat," yelled Rob. "You got a head start." She slowed down, allowing him to catch her. Grabbing her hand, he ran beside her to Mary's truck.

"Rob, get my razor and shaving cream, will you?" Dad called from his bedroom.

Rob pulled himself out of the soft sofa cushions and started back toward the bathroom. He took the shaving gear from the medicine chest behind the mirror. Standing in the doorway to his father's room, he tossed them onto the bed beside the suitcase, right on top of Dad's good blue suit. Of course there was to be partying as well as horse buying. He walked back toward the living room.

"Thanks," Dad said to Rob's retreating back.

In the living room, Rob again flopped down on the couch. He picked up a copy of *Hoof Beats* that lay on the coffee table.

"Rob?"

Rob threw the magazine forcefully onto the table and prepared to answer yet another of his father's requests, but Dad was coming to him.

"Here's the name and number of the motel where I'll be staying." Dad pinned the note to the small corkboard in the kitchen next to the phone. "Call if anything comes up." As

Rob again picked up the magazine, Dad opened the refrigerator, taking a beer. "Want anything?" he asked.

"Yeah—a beer," Rob answered sarcastically.

"Well, why not?" Dad said. He grabbed another beer, and, coming back into the living room, handed it to Rob. "One won't hurt you, and the way I look at it, you're going to be doing a man's job while I'm away, so you're entitled."

Rob didn't even want the damned beer. He tore the tab from the top and tossed it across the living room, barely making a basket in the trash can.

"I really appreciate having you here, Rob. It's nice to have family to keep an eye on the stable while I'm gone."

"Yeah, sure. That's why you put Frank in charge."

Dad sat down next to him, giving Rob's knee a friendly slap. "Heck, Frank's in charge in name only. The other grooms will listen to him. But I've told him he's not your boss. He'll be there if you need him. You're my partner, man, and as soon as I get back, we'll get things going toward getting your license. How's that?"

Was Dad just B.S.ing him or did he mean it? Rob wanted to believe him. "That's cool, Dad. And listen, tonight I'll stick around after feeding time to make sure the barn's closed for the night, all right?"

"That's great—but remember, Frank's getting paid to manage the stable." Dad fished in his pants pocket and pulled out his keys. He handed them to Rob. "Here are the keys to the truck and the trailer. Have a good time. Why don't you ask that cute little Kylie out?" Dad chuckled and winked at him.

"Maybe I will." Rob tossed the keys into the air, caught them, and then slipped them into his jeans pocket.

Dad was giving Rob his final instructions when they were interrupted by the blare of a car horn.

"That must be Vic Barrone," Dad said. "Tell him I'm coming, while I get my suitcase."

Rob opened the trailer door. But Mr. Barrone wasn't waiting for Dad. His daughter, Nicole, sat in the pale blue Thunderbird convertible in front of the trailer. "He's coming," Rob said flatly. He went back into the living room, closing the door behind him.

Dad came out of the bedroom with his suitcase and a sportcoat over his arm. "Well, come on," he said as he opened the door. "Walk your old man out to the car and meet Mr. Barrone."

Dad was out the door before Rob could tell him that Mr. Barrone wasn't there. With a sigh, he shuffled after Dad.

"Well, look who's here," said Dad, obviously delighted.

"Hi," Nicole said. "Daddy had to run some papers into his office, so he said he'd meet us at the airport."

"That's fine with me," said Dad, winking at Nicole.

"Hi, Robbie," Nicole said in a tone girls usually reserved for boys under the age of five.

Although it seemed necessary to raise his hand in greeting, Rob quickly let it drop to his side. He looked at Dad. "Have a good time," he said.

Dad gave him an embarrassed embrace before slipping into the passenger seat of the car.

"This is going to be so much fun," bubbled Nicole. "I've never been to a horse sale."

"It's something to see," said Dad.

Rob had never been to a horse sale, either.

"You know where to reach me, Rob. I'll see you on Thursday," Dad said as Nicole started the car.

Rob watched the car roll away from him. He waved, but Dad was deep in conversation with Nicole. He could see Dad's smiling silhouette through the rear window. Rob waved harder. Dad didn't turn back to him. Rob's chest began to constrict and his breathing came rapidly. His instinct was to chase the car like he'd done when he was six, the time Dad had exploded out of the trailer during a fight with Mom. Rob had been playing in front and had watched him jump into his truck and speed away. Crying, Rob had run after him all the way to the park entrance, where Ernie had grabbed him before he could chase Dad down the road.

Rob watched the Thunderbird turn onto the road. He was alone again. But he was sixteen now. He didn't need Dad. He sure didn't need Ernie either.

Rob went back into the trailer and flipped on the TV. A sheriff was ready to face down a gang of bad guys in the middle of a street that was obviously on some backlot set of a cheap studio. He changed the channel: stock car races . . . *National Geographic* at the South Pole . . . a bowling tournament. Great.

He went to the refrigerator. He was going to Mary's for dinner in a few hours. He didn't want to go smelling like a brewery, so he passed up the beer and grabbed an orange drink. He sat uneasily on the edge of a chair at the kitchen table and looked out the window at the car lot. It was busy, but the sight of all those people bustling from car to car only made him more edgy.

He checked the clock. One hour until feeding time, two-and-a-half until he was due at Mary's. Rob began to pace. He wasn't supposed to feel like this here, not with Dad. Sure, at Granddad's he got these weird feelings, especially when he was in the house alone. He'd never told them. Mom didn't give a crap anyway and would just bitch at him about being grateful. And Granddad would only fuss around and insist on Rob's going everywhere with him. More golf he didn't need. Besides, a few beers usually dulled the panic. But here? He'd come home. Why did he feel so caged? Rob tossed the drink box into the trash and darted for the door, locking it behind him. He was getting out of there.

When he pulled up in front of the barn, he still had forty minutes to kill before feeding time. Well, there was always something to be done at a stable. He went first to Tessa's stall. She had rolled in manure. After cleaning the stall, Rob got her brushes and started to work on her.

"Tessa, you are a mess," he said, brushing the now-dried manure from her shoulder. The filly leaned into his hand. She loved to be brushed, and as Rob came closer to her head, she stretched her neck to nuzzle his shoulder. Rob rubbed her nose, smiling. "I like you, too," he said. He brushed down her legs and over her back. He brought the currycomb up to the base of her tail and rubbed in small circles. The filly stretched her nose into the air, her lip curled, her head bobbing as if in ecstasy. Rob laughed.

"Whoa, Robbie, who you got in there?" Dusty peered into the stall. From Dusty's bloodshot eyes and the mellow expression on his gaunt face, it was obvious how he'd spent his afternoon.

"Dusty, do you always stay high? Don't you ever come down?"

"Not if I can help it, buddy," Dusty laughed shrilly. "We're all getting together behind Barn Five about nine. It'll help beat the weekend blahs. Hell, there's nothing else to do around here on Sundays once the matinee races are over. What do you say?"

"Not tonight."

"It's all right. Beak went to Batavia today. He won't be back until late."

"I'm not afraid of Beak."

Dusty shuffled his feet and looked uneasy. "Listen, Rob, you should be. I know I thought it was cool when you pulverized him, but he was really drunk that night. He's been talking awfully big about what he's going to do to you."

"Come on, Dusty. I can handle Beak."

"Yeah, but you gotta know he carries a knife. Now as far as I know, he's never cut nobody with it, but it's always in his pocket."

"Well, I won't be at the party tonight, but Beak has nothing to do with it. I'm going out to dinner and I don't think I'll be back early."

"You know where we'll be if you do get back," Dusty said, before going to feed his horses.

One by one the other grooms wandered in to feed their horses. And one by one they wandered off when the job was done, leaving Rob and Frank.

Rob decided to take Dad's advice and let Frank close up. He was due soon at Mary's and had barely enough time to wash up and change his shirt. "I'll see you in the morning, Frank," Rob said, heading for the grooms' quarters.

He unlocked the door and went in, closing it behind him. He could hear a radio playing in the room behind and someone laughing next door. The tiny room felt snug, comfortable. He slipped one of Dad's shirts, a pale-blue knit, from its hanger. Grabbing a washrag and towel, he headed for the bathroom.

The bathroom smelled—mold, wet concrete, urine, soap, and cheap after-shave. A young groom Rob recognized as working for the stable behind theirs emerged from the shower, wrapped in a towel. "Hey, Walsh," he said. "What's doing?"

"Not much," Rob answered.

The boy moved to the sink, where he'd left his after-shave and comb. "Well, I've got a hot date tonight," said the boy, combing his hair. "With every other night a race night, Sunday's the only night to go out."

Maybe next Sunday Rob would ask Kylie out. Maybe he wouldn't wait if he had a free night during the week.

Back in the room, Rob picked up his dirty shirt and stashed it in the small laundry basket under the bed. He turned on the radio, changing Dad's country station to the local FM rock channel. Checking the dresser drawer, he found clean underwear, a pair of khakis, and handkerchiefs. He pocketed a handkerchief. Laughter—the woman's light and melodious, the man's deep and full—drifted from the room next door. A girl started to sing with the radio in the room behind his.

Tomorrow Rob would bring some of his things from the trailer. He was staying here until Dad came back.

8

Rob stopped the truck in front of the farm's Kentucky gate. Before pulling the chain to open it, he pushed Dad's sunglasses up on his nose and ran his fingers through his hair so that it flopped across his forehead. He checked out his appearance in the rearview mirror to see if he really looked as cool as he thought he did. Not bad. He looked like the kind of guy who'd drive an amazing truck like this.

He opened and closed the gate like he'd seen Dad do. Then, lounging against the door with his arm out the window, he let the truck roll toward the house. But no one came out of the house to greet him, not even after he let the engine rumble a few minutes. He drove toward the new barn, but no one came to greet him there, either. "Hey, anybody home?" he yelled.

Mary stuck her head out of the lab door. "In here, Rob," she called.

When Rob joined her in the lab, he found her arranging tiny medicine bottles on a shelf. "A big order came in yesterday and we didn't have time to put it away," she said.

Rob wanted to ask her where Kylie was, but he didn't want to be teased, so he picked up a box from a nearby table and carried it to the counter. "Where does this go?" he asked.

"That's the last box, so it must be the diuretic. Second shelf."

Rob stepped beside her and began placing the bottles on the shelf.

"Did your Dad get off all right?"

"Yeah," he answered. He glanced at Mary, who was looking at him with her forehead furrowed. "What's the matter?"

"Nothing, really. I was trying to think of some way to be tactful, and you know how hard that is for me."

Was she going to play Kylie's protective aunt?

"Tact is sometimes just an excuse to avoid tough issues, and since I may not have a chance to speak to you alone later, I might as well have a go at it." She took a deep breath and turned to face him. "Kylie tells me you're thinking of staying here with your dad, becoming his partner."

"I've been thinking about it."

Mary pressed her lips together. Rob could feel the weight of her disapproval pressing against him in the confinement of the lab. Why was she making such a big deal out of this? Mom and Granddad he expected to fuss. But Mary?

"Rob, the horse business is a tough way to make a living. You know that. Your Dad may be having a good year, but how many bad years has he had, and what guarantees does he have that next year won't be the worst yet?"

"Dad had some bad breaks—Pap dying, and then everybody pulling out on him before he could prove himself. But if I start young, I can build my reputation early. I'll have a better chance of making it."

"Everybody in this business has a tale of bad years. Some

people seem to be able to minimize them, but everybody has them. I'm not even sure that's my real concern."

"Ah, Mary, you're starting to sound like Mom."

"This would flip out your mom, wouldn't it? Is that why you're thinking of it? And if not, then you tell me why."

"I don't know. I want to. Do I have to have a reason besides that?" Mary still stared at him, demanding more. Rob went back to arranging the diuretics on the shelf. Mary took his wrist in one of her strong, short-fingered hands and turned him back to face her.

"Look, you know I never could keep my mouth shut if I had something to say. I won't tell you the business is no good for you. I love it too much—and you wouldn't believe me anyway. If it's right for you, you'll know it, but it takes time to be sure. Too many people choose this business because it's an easy way to drop out. The track has everything you need—food, lodging, employment, entertainment, and companion-ship—all within the gates. Make sure you're not just hiding out, Rob."

"Come on, Mary, you know I'm good with horses." He didn't want to be angry with Mary, but she didn't have any right to tell him what to do. "Look, I've always wanted to be part of this business."

"No, you haven't. I distinctly remember you telling me when you were about three that you wanted to grow up to be Big Bird. Frankly, today you're more like Oscar the Grouch." Mary's laugh broke the tension.

"I'm sorry I snapped, Mary. Let's talk about something else, okay?"

"Agreed," said Mary. "Besides, I've said my piece—for now." She placed the last bottle from Rob's box on the shelf and shut the cupboard. "Michael and Kylie will be back soon.

They went to church at St. Anthony's. I'm just going to throw some steaks on the grill for dinner, but I want to get the potatoes started before they come home. Come on. You can help."

As they walked onto the porch, the phone began to ring. Mary darted ahead to answer it. Rob followed and heard her giving advice on a cracked hoof. He tapped her on the shoulder and pointed toward the stallion paddocks so she would know where to find him.

So Kylie was Catholic. Rob remembered St. Anthony's Church and himself as a young boy in a crisp, white suit standing in line to receive his first Holy Communion. Pap and Gram had thrown a big party for him afterward. But he couldn't remember when they had quit going to church. Granddad went—not every Sunday, but often and on every Christmas and Easter—to the big, white-spired Presbyterian church in the city. Sometimes he asked if Rob wanted to come with him, but Rob never did. Strange, he never thought about church anymore.

When he reached the paddocks, Rob whistled. Rat ran to the fence in response, and for a minute Rob was glad that Kylie wasn't there—that he had been able to summon the big horse for himself. Stopping in front of Rob, Rat nudged him with his nose, searching for carrots. Without them, Rat only tolerated Rob's attention for a few moments before bolting, pacing to the far end of the paddock. Rob perched on the top board of the fence, watching the horse as he rolled in a patch of dirt. Rob concentrated on Rat, on the hot sun beating down on the back of his shirt, and on the earthy horse smell permeating the barn area, freeing himself from the annoying questions Mary had asked.

"Rob, hello," Kylie called, walking toward him, the stark

white of her sundress showing off her tanned arms and legs. There was a glow to her smooth, tawny skin and looseness to her movement that drove away any thought that wasn't of her.

"Kylie," he called, jumping down to meet her and not caring that he'd left the sunglasses in the truck.

"Mary's getting dinner ready and Michael's in his studio. I want to show you something," she said, turning back toward the house.

"What are you going to show me?" Rob asked, falling in step beside her.

"A surprise. You'll love it," she answered. "It's in the studio."

They entered the studio through the back door. A pungent smell that was a mixture of shellac, linseed oil, and stripping compounds assailed Rob's nose as they stepped into the workshop. Sunlight flooded through floor-to-ceiling windows on one side of the room. Wood was everywhere—small chunks on the shelves, huge blocks on the floor. In the center of the room was a huge worktable. Kylie led the way to the table, where a space had been cleared in the clutter. In the space stood a half-finished carving.

Rob stepped closer. From a block of red wood about the size of half a shoebox emerged the head, neck, back, and shoulders of a horse. The horse's mane seemed to be dancing away from his powerful neck in a fierce wind. The cut of the head and the set of the eye was unmistakable. "It's Rat, isn't it?"

Kylie nodded. "Isn't it wonderful?"

Before Rob could answer, Michael entered the workshop. "Michael, this is amazing. Even the color of the wood is exactly the color of Rat's coat."

"When the man who finds me my rare woods showed me

this piece of Honduran mahogany, all I could see in it was that goofy stallion. I know Kylie's fond of him, and I wanted her to take something of mine home with her this fall." He ran one finger tenderly over the back of the carving. "I see him like one of those Chinese Lei T'ai horses—in a free-flying pace suspended about the base. What do you think?"

Rob didn't feel worthy of offering an opinion, but he could see the carving as Michael described it. "It would make him seem less free if his feet were on a base, wouldn't it?"

"That's what I thought," Michael answered.

Rob looked around the room. On a shelf against a brick wall were many wooden bowls. Rob lifted a large, free-form bowl from a shelf. It was carved from a black-and-white striped wood. "I've never seen a wood like this," Rob said. The streaks in the wood ranged from white to ivory to gray to jet. Rob ran a hand down one side of the bowl from the carefully rounded elliptical rim to the narrow, round base. The wood beneath his fingers was satiny smooth and cool.

"That's for an old friend who owns an antique mall. I've done his refinishing for years. I wanted him to have something I made, as well as all the things I've repaired and refinished," Michael said.

For the first time, Rob noticed the old dressers and tables and chairs in the corners of the room. In one corner stood a gleaming dresser of wood nearly as red as the carving of Rat.

"Those old pieces will all look as good as that dresser when Michael's finished with them," Kylie said proudly.

Rob placed the bowl carefully back on its shelf. "Michael, how long have you been doing this?" With a sweep of his arm, he included all the work in the room.

"A wood shop course I took as a senior in high school got me started. At first, I did birdhouses. We had a birdhouse hanging from darn near every branch of every tree in our yard. Soon I was carving designs on the birdhouses, and then I was carving figures and making furniture. I've tried doing other things—I have a degree in accounting. But I always come back to my wood. I'm not happy if I don't."

"That's because it's your gift," Kylie said. "And you can't deny a gift."

"I think most gifts are 90 percent perspiration and practice," Michael said. "Maybe the ability to see the beauty in it and the desire to create that kind of beauty are gifts."

"Michael, if I could do work like this," Rob said, "I'd never do anything else." He thought of how Dad had tried to minimize Michael's work. Maybe Dad had never even seen it. But then, Rob couldn't imagine Dad taking the time to look.

"Well, why don't you come and spend some time with me?" said Michael. "I'll teach you the basics."

"Oh, Rob, that would be neat," bubbled Kylie.

Instantly, Rob was leery. Had he been set up? First Mary's lecture. Now Michael offering to teach him woodworking. "I don't know, Michael," Rob stammered. He looked at Kylie, who stared steadily at him. He didn't really believe she was that conniving. Neither was Mary—she had merely told him what was on her mind. But this sure did look like a setup. "I don't know if I'll have time, Michael," he said.

"I promised Mary I'd make the salad for dinner," Kylie said, linking her arm in Rob's, pulling him after her toward the door. "And Rob, I told her you'd help me."

"In that case," said Michael, "I'd better finish up here, because dinner should be about ready."

Rob looked around the studio again. He'd probably stink at wood carving, anyway.

9

The track was dark and quiet when Rob drove in that night.
The security guard at the gate didn't even get up from his
chair before waving Rob through. At the ends of each barn,
vapor lamps glowed like private moons.

The clock on the truck's dash showed just after ten—too
early for bed. Besides, Rob wasn't ready to shut himself in
yet. He should have asked Kylie if she wanted to go out to a
movie or something, but when they had a few minutes alone
and the time was right, the words wouldn't come. He'd call
her tomorrow. Maybe they could go out tomorrow night.

Instead of turning toward the grooms' quarters, Rob turned
left to the stable. He'd check the horses before going to bed.

As he stepped from the truck, he heard a banging and
thrashing coming from one of the stalls. Rob ran to the shed
row. He turned on the barn lights, and the thrashing became
wilder—from Tessa's stall. Rob threw open the stall door.
Tessa was cast. She had rolled over too close to the wall and,
with her legs pinned between her belly and the wall, she
couldn't extend them to roll back or to stand. "Easy now,

Tess," Rob whispered. As he approached her head, Tessa panicked, flailing her legs madly in an effort to stand. She must have been pinned like this for some time, Rob realized. She was a mess—her face was covered with blood from banging it against the floor and the wall. "Whoa, now," Rob said softly. "You're going to be all right, girl." He grabbed the top of her halter and pulled. Her front end slid on the straw a few feet. Quickly, he grabbed her tail and pulled her hind feet away from the wall.

Tessa immediately leapt to her feet and shied to the back of the stall, where she stood trembling, dark with sweat. Both front knees were rubbed raw and bloody, most of the skin was off her muzzle, and blood streamed down her face from a long gash over her right eye.

Now Rob began to tremble. What should he do? Call Mary? Maybe Tessa was all right, just scraped up a bit. No, too much blood. But maybe there was only a lot of blood and no serious damage. He stepped toward Tessa and she cringed away, trembling more violently.

A blanket. She could get a chill. Rob got the blanket from her trunk. "Come on, Tess, let me have a look at you," he coaxed, walking slowly toward her. She let him grasp her halter before she spooked, dragging Rob toward the front of the stall. With one hand on her halter and the other stroking her neck, he managed to calm her enough to fasten her in the cross ties.

Rob ran his hands down her legs, always the first worry with a race horse. The knees were cut superficially, but were already swollen. The gash over her eye was deep and still oozing blood. It probably needed to be stitched, and Rob was sure the eye should be examined. He unfastened the cross ties so she wouldn't feel confined and panic while he was gone.

Feeling in his pocket for a quarter, he ran to the pay phone on the porch of the administration building. He couldn't remember Mary's number—737-something. Information. Rob dialed and the operator gave him the number. His fingers seemed slow and clumsy as they dialed.

"This is Mary Tanner. I am not able to answer the phone right now," came the recorded message.

"Mary, pick up the phone," Rob wailed. "I know you're there."

"Rob, is that you?" said Mary, interrupting her machine.

"Mary, Tessa's hurt. She was cast when I got back. Her knees are racked up and there's a bad gash above her eye."

"I'm on my way, Rob." The phone went dead.

Tessa was still shaking and sweat was running down her flanks when Rob got back to the stall. "We'll get you cleaned up a little, Tess," he said, going for a bucket. After filling the bucket with warm water and throwing in some clean cloths, Rob fastened her again in the cross ties and went to work.

By the time Rob had the blood cleaned off her face and knees, Mary and Kylie arrived.

Mary rushed into the stall first, with Kylie behind her. "Okay," Mary said, "let's have a look at her."

Kylie came to Rob's side and they watched Mary examining the filly. When Mary tried to touch the gash over her eye, Tessa tossed her head and began shaking again. "I'm going to have to suture that gash, so I'd better give her something to calm her. She's still pretty fussed up," Mary said, heading for her truck. She returned with a hypodermic. "Easy, Tessa," she soothed, inserting the needle into the filly's neck. "Come on, Kylie, let's get my suture kit and leave the filly alone with Rob. We'll give that shot some time to work."

Left alone with Tessa, Rob stroked her neck and talked softly to her. Gradually, the trembling stopped. By the time Mary and Kylie returned, Tessa seemed relaxed, even a little sleepy.

Mary probed the wound over Tessa's eye. "It's a deep one, all right," she said. "Kylie, you get over on her left side and hold onto her halter. Grab an ear to distract her from what I'm doing. Rob, this is still bleeding a little, so I want you to sponge for me." She handed him a small surgical sponge. "We'll be right in front of her eye, and at least she knows you. When I say 'sponge,' lightly press the sponge on the area I'm suturing. Got it?"

Rob nodded. The sight of blood had never bothered him, but then he'd never had to help with anything like this. After injecting Novocaine around the wound, Mary began to stitch. The sight of the needle piercing Tessa's flesh gave Rob a momentary twinge. "Sponge." Rob brought the sponge gently down onto the wound. Stitch. "Sponge." Stitch. "Sponge."

Tessa stood quietly. Mary's hands were steady and capable and, so, Rob realized, were his. The precision with which Mary stitched the open gash amazed him. She was so confident, so sure; the ugly gash closed under her deft work. "Sponge and we're done," Mary said after the tenth suture. "Kylie, get me the antibiotic and the tetanus antitoxin."

Blood still oozed from between the stitches and Rob sponged it away. He looked at Mary standing outside the stall, taking the bottles from Kylie. Mary looked as triumphant and satisfied as he felt. She probably often felt like this, experiencing not just the satisfaction of "a job well done," as Granddad would say, but the deep, exhilarating satisfaction of knowing she had helped—she had made a difference.

Mary came into the stall and moved back to the filly's neck to give her the injections. Rob watched as Mary and Kylie then cleaned Tessa's knees and examined her legs. "Well, her head seems to have taken the worst of it," said Mary. She took her flashlight out of her pocket and shone it in Tessa's eyes. "She doesn't seem to have damaged her eyes. She's lucky you came when you did."

The call-buzzer clipped to Mary's belt went off. "What now?" she mumbled, going to her truck and the mobile phone unit.

"The stitching didn't bother you at all, did it?" Kylie asked.

"Not after the first stitch," he answered proudly.

"My toes curl with every stitch. The blood doesn't bother me, but that needle going into flesh does. Mary says I'll get used to it, but I'm not so sure."

Rob grinned, happy to be able to do something Kylie found difficult.

"Emergency in Barn Twelve," said Mary, returning. "A gelding with colic."

"Ask if you can stay with me until she's done," Rob whispered to Kylie.

"Rob," said Mary, "Tessa doesn't need to be in the cross ties. You can let her loose, but keep an eye on her for a while longer. I'll stop back before I leave the track."

"Mary, may I stay here with Rob, or do you think you'll need my help?" Kylie asked.

"Sure, you can stay. The gelding's groom is there to help me. Although I must say, I don't think it will take the two of you to watch one little filly."

Feeling very sure of himself after all the events of the evening, Rob took Kylie's hand and led her to the tack trunk by Tessa's stall so they could watch the filly. Kylie bounced onto the trunk, sitting close to him. The warmth Rob had been feeling grew.

"It always amazes me how peaceful this place is at night when there's no racing. Especially since most of the time it's such a zoo," said Kylie.

"When I was a little kid, sometimes I was allowed to stay up late to help Dad close the barn for the night. After everyone else would leave our barn, I always felt like we were the only two people left on the whole track. I knew it wasn't so, but it still made me feel like we owned the place," said Rob.

"It must have been hard when you had to leave."

"When we left here, at least we went to another track. It was harder when Mom decided she'd had enough of this 'gypsy life,' as she called it. When I first went to Granddad's, I was still waking up every morning thinking I had to go help Dad feed the horses."

Kylie said nothing, but leaned into Rob's shoulder. Rob dropped the hand he had been holding, slipping his arm around her. She nestled into his shoulder, and he liked how her shoulder seemed to fit so perfectly under his own. Her face was close to his. Leaning forward, he kissed her. Before he could kiss her again, she smiled and leaned back against the barn wall. His arm still around her, Rob leaned back, too, moving his arm to the crook of her neck, hoping to position himself to kiss her again.

"I'm sorry I didn't say anything when you told me about leaving with your mom," Kylie said. "It's just because it's so sad, and I never know what to say when someone tells me something sad." Had she only kissed him because she felt sorry for him? "When I was ten, my parents were having a lot of arguments about my mom going back to school," Kylie continued. "I was sure they were going to divorce. I'd lie awake at night trying to decide who I wanted to live with. I was scared to death. Anyway, they weren't really having serious troubles, and I didn't have to choose. Neither did Mom. She'll be graduated from college next spring."

"Well, I wasn't given a choice," Rob said sourly. He didn't want to keep talking.

"Do you think you would have chosen to stay with your dad?"

"I don't know. Maybe. I would now."

"What's your mother like?"

"I don't know," Rob said brusquely.

"I'm sorry. It's none of my business," Kylie said, looking hurt.

"Kylie, I wasn't trying to shut you out," Rob said, although in a way he was. He didn't like to talk about his parents, about the divorce, about himself, but there had been more to his answer than that. "I really don't know what my mother is like. I mean, I used to, but she's not like she used to be and now she's never around. Granddad bought into this real estate company for her. She works all the time, so I don't see her much." Kylie was looking at him sympathetically again, and that wasn't what he wanted from her. "Every kid's dream, huh? Who wants their mother around all the time?" Rob forced a laugh, but the warm, good feelings he'd had were disappearing.

"What about your granddad?"

"If I could just get him out of the house when Mom's gone, everything would be perfect. But not Granddad. He makes sure we have dinner together, even if he has to go out in the evening. In nice weather we usually eat at his country club, and then he insists on a round of golf after dinner. He just can't accept that I'm rotten at golf and don't care that I am. He considers a good golf game a prime asset for all businessmen. Of course, he can't accept that I'm not going to be a businessman, either—that I have no intention of joining him in the family food business." Rob felt his body stiffen in spite of his efforts to keep his voice and posture cool.

Kylie snuggled closer to him, putting her arms around his chest. "At least you don't have to be lonely if you have your grandfather there."

But most of the time he was lonely, and now even with Kylie's arms around him, he was again feeling lonely and cold. He looked at Kylie, hoping she could read his need. She smiled, hugging him, and the wonderful warmth started to return. Rob rubbed his hand along the firm, rounded flesh where her arm met her shoulder. Still she smiled. He pulled her to him, pressing his mouth against hers. She returned his kiss. He kissed her again and again. The cold was gone, but the heat that was replacing it made him even more desperate. He squeezed her more tightly to him. As long as he held her, he would be fine. The cold would not return and she could soothe the burning.

But Kylie was trying to pull away. No! She had to feel what he did. He thrust his tongue against her teeth, and, still holding her securely with one arm, felt for her breast with his other hand.

Kylie struggled against him. "Rob, stop it," she gasped, putting both of her hands against his shoulders and pushing him away so forcefully that his back hit the barn wall.

Confused and embarrassed, he could only mumble, "You wanted me to kiss you."

Kylie, red-faced, leapt to her feet. "Yes, I wanted you to kiss me, but I didn't want to get jumped." She straightened her clothing.

She was a tease. She'd just been playing him along. Well, who needed her? "Why? Because you're such a good little girl?"

"You're lucky that I'm a good little girl or you'd be picking your teeth out of your tonsils about now, you jerk." She wiped her eyes on the back of her hand as she turned and strode away from him.

She was leaving. Well, he didn't need her. He didn't need anybody. "Screw you," Rob yelled after her.

Kylie stopped and turned toward him, glaring. "It was my impression that's what you were trying to do."

And then she was gone, disappearing in the direction of Barn Twelve. Rob was alone again except for Tessa, who was calmly munching hay.

Beyond the reach of the barn lights the night was dark. Rob shivered and, nervously rubbing his arms to keep himself warm, ventured into the darkness to find Dusty and the party he'd been told about.

10

Rob tossed three dollars into the can by the beer tub. He reached for a beer, but before he could take a sip, Dusty and Sue Ellen came running up to him.

"You gotta get out of here, man," Dusty whispered. "Beak's back. He's bombed and crazy." Sue Ellen kept nodding her head, her eyes wide.

"I told you, Dusty, I'm not afraid of Beak," Rob said, but felt a cold tingling of fear at the base of his spine. If Beak did really carry a knife, that changed the odds.

Beak came lurching toward them. "Who in the hell invited you here, Walsh? You're really pushing your luck. I ain't as drunk as I was the other night." Beak took a step toward Rob. Beak's bloodshot eyes looked wild, not the effect of booze alone.

"Back off, Beak," said Rob. "I'm not here to bother you."

"Just your being here bothers me," Beak snarled.

"Come on, Beak," Dixie broke in, "leave him alone and let's go have some fun." She flung her arms around Beak, rubbing his chest.

Beak allowed Dixie to lead him away. "I'll deal with you later, scum bucket," he yelled at Rob.

Rob wasn't up to this. He grabbed a six-pack from the tub and headed for his room.

Mary's truck sat beside his barn and the light was on in Tessa's stall when Rob sneaked by. Good. Now he wouldn't have to stop and check the filly. Kylie could just come looking for him if anything was wrong.

Alone in the room, Rob downed his opened beer and grabbed one from the six-pack. He turned on the radio. Two beers later, he was still alone. His room number was posted on the blackboard by the feed room; Kylie and Mary could have found him if they needed him.

Someone began to pound on the metal door to Rob's room. His heart sank—something was wrong with Tessa. But then it must be Kylie at the door. With mixed emotions, he jumped to his feet. "Walsh, you dirty little son of a bitch, open this door," Beak shouted. The pounding came again, deafeningly loud in the concrete-block cubicle. Rob froze as the doorknob turned back and forth. Thank God he'd locked the door.

"Beak, baby, come away from there," Rob heard Dixie say, trying again to distract Beak.

The sound of boots kicking the door now filled the room. Rob stayed quiet. Only a fool would fight a guy who had a knife. "You cowardly bastard," Beak yelled, "I'll get you yet." And then there was silence.

Rob sank onto the bed, breathing deeply for some minutes before creeping to the high square window beside the door. Carefully, he lifted a corner of the shade to peek out. Beak was gone. Rob flopped back onto his bed. Whether his stomach ached from fear or from three beers too quickly downed, he didn't know. What if he had to vomit? He already had to go to the bathroom, but he sure didn't want to leave his room.

As he lay on his bed the nausea passed, but his need to urinate only became more insistent. There was no doubt about it—he was going to have to go to the bathroom. Before opening the door, he peeked out of the window. The coast was clear.

It was only about twenty-five feet from Rob's door to the bathrooms. He made it at a fast walk, unseen. When he finished, he peered out of the stall before making his escape. Someone was coming. As he ducked back into the stall, he heard someone fall against the swinging door that separated the shower area from the toilets. Whoever it was headed toward him. The stalls were without doors and Rob was sure to be seen.

" 'Oh, Lawd, won't you buy me a Mercedes-Benz?' " a decidedly female voice sang. What was a woman doing in the men's room? Dixie staggered by the stall in which Rob hid. He should have known. But where was Beak? He could be right behind her or still waiting in his room or, perhaps, on his way to find her. The safest course seemed to be to wait it out. He waited quietly until Dixie finished using the toilet in the next stall.

But on her way out, she spotted him. Her eyes widened, looking frightened. "Rob, what are you doing in here?" she whispered.

"This is the men's room. What are you doing here?"

"The women's room is in the next building. I never would have made it," she laughed, loudly.

"Shhh," urged Rob.

" '*Shhh*' is right! Beak'll kill you if he finds you in here. You better go," she said, her eyes darting toward the door as if she heard footsteps.

They both started for the door. Beak's room was in the row

that backed into Rob's. Dixie should have been using the other door, but she was following Rob. As he turned to ask her why, her bare feet slipped on a wet place near the showers. Rob reached to catch her as she fell, but he slipped, too, and fell on top of her. Quickly, he jumped to his feet, but Dixie still lay on the floor, her torn, pink cotton robe open, revealing her naked body. If Beak came now, Rob was double dead. He reached down to help her to her feet and noticed tears in her eyes.

"Are you all right?" he asked.

"Sure. I bumped my head and it hurts is all," she said, rubbing the back of her head.

Rob felt her head. There was an egg coming, but not a big one. "Look," he said, "you're headed the wrong way—Beak's room's on the other side."

She pulled away from him. "I'm not going back to Beak's room. I'm going to mine. He's on a mean drunk and he's scaring me." She looked like she was going to cry.

Rob patted her arm. Her room wasn't even in this row—it was in the grooms' quarters on the opposite side of the stable area, and she was planning on walking there barefoot and half naked.

"Dixie, you whore, where are you?" Beak bellowed. A door slammed.

"Oh, no," she cried, grabbing Rob's arm. "Get me out of here, please. He'll kill both of us."

Rob took her hand and ran for his room. As they raced out the door, he heard Beak entering the bathroom by the opposite door yelling, "You had better answer me! I mean it!"

Rob slammed the door to his room behind them, locking it. Dixie sank onto the bed. Rob, feeling uncomfortable, sat on the floor.

"That was a close one," sighed Dixie. "You got anything to drink, sweet lips?"

Rob tossed her one of the remaining beers. She held it for a moment on the back of her head before opening it and taking a sip. Rob helped himself to a beer. "Does your head still hurt?" he asked.

"No, I'm fine," she answered.

Rob went back to drinking his beer. He heard footsteps in the gravel outside his door. They seemed to hesitate. Rob looked at Dixie, who held her fingers to her lips, signaling silence. She looked so frightened that Rob got angry. That beady-eyed bastard. Who did he think he was? Rob started to get to his feet, but Dixie shook her head and pushed him back down. The footsteps moved on.

"He's going to my room. I know he is. And he'll be back when he doesn't find me," Dixie said, sniffing as if she was about to cry.

"Dixie, I'm not up to a crying jag so, please, don't start one," Rob said. "Beak's a jerk. Everyone knows it. Why don't you just tell him to get lost?"

"Most of the time he's not so bad. He's better than the last guy I was with." She took a long drink from her can of beer. "What the hell, it beats being alone."

"I don't understand you," he mumbled, taking a drink. Heck, he was lonely, too, but he wouldn't let himself be treated so badly. She was pathetic.

"You don't have to understand me, sugar. Just get me another beer, and maybe later we can have us some fun." Dixie wiggled back against the wall, her robe pulling up to reveal her blue-veined legs and thighs.

Rob tossed her one of the last two beers. The other he kept for himself. He studied her, considering what she offered. His groin ached at the thought, but the look Dixie gave him wasn't a come-on. She looked frightened—of him. He thought of all the stray dogs, motherless kittens, and fledgling birds he'd dragged home since he was four or five, always to his mother's horror. Well, what would Mom think of what he'd brought home tonight? He gave a short laugh. "Relax, Dix. I don't want to screw you. I just want to get drunk, and I'm not sure I'm going to be able to do that with this one last beer." Normally, five beers would have fixed him up fine, but Beak had had a sobering effect on him.

Tears came again to Dixie's eyes. "Rob, you really *are* a nice guy. Not many guys have given me free drinks." She laughed suddenly, and jumped to her feet. "Wait here," she called, and before Rob could stop her, she darted out the door. Rob followed, peering from the open door as she slipped into the bathroom. Jeez, what was she doing? Rob stepped outside, looking in the direction he expected Beak would come. No one was in sight.

"We're in business," Dixie called, emerging from the bathroom only seconds later with three cans of beer.

"Dixie, you are certifiably nuts," Rob said. "If those are Beak's, you can bet he'll miss them."

She pushed past into the room and he locked the door behind her. "I left him three. That's fair," she said.

Rob only sipped at one beer and let Dixie guzzle the other two. She slipped a capsule from the pocket of her tattered robe and downed it with her last sip of beer. "I can't sleep without them," she mumbled. Soon she nestled into Rob's pillow and shut her eyes.

"Hey, Dixie! Wait a minute! Where am I going to sleep?" Rob asked. But she was already snoring. He sat watching her sleep, the faded pink ruffles of her robe against her cheek.

He knew her reputation. The rumor was she'd sleep with anyone for a can of beer. Rob guessed that was mostly true.

She moaned in her sleep. Rob lifted the lightweight blanket from the foot of his bed and covered her. She woke, startled, and stared at him with wild eyes, cowering. She looked like Tessa had earlier in the evening—afraid of more pain. "It's all right, Dixie. It's me—Rob. No one's going to hurt you." He patted her arm as she snuggled back into the pillow and slept.

Rob pulled some blankets from the footlocker under the bed and the extra pillow from the shelf overhead. The concrete floor made a hard bed, but that was all right—he didn't mind.

Where in the hell had Dixie gone? Rob looked around the room, trying to clear his brain. Wait. That was Sunday night she'd stayed in his room. But what had happened last night?

Rob tried to sit up, but a pain shot through his head. He leaned back against his pillow. *Think through the fuzzies*, he commanded himself. Right. Last night—a party, beer, whiskey, grass . . . Now he remembered: he'd taken Dixie to a party last night. Beak hadn't been around. They'd both gotten wrecked. But where was she now? How could he take care of her if she ran off like this?

No, she was fine. He'd walked her to her room and made sure she'd locked the door after herself. Then he had a vague memory of going back to the party, but he didn't remember how he'd ended up in his own room in bed.

Rob buried his head in his pillow, hoping its softness would ease the throbbing. He looked at the alarm clock. It wasn't even six yet. He rubbed his hand across his forehead. His head hurt too much for him to get back to sleep.

Slowly, Rob rose from his bed, pushing away the dingy,

twisted sheet. He had to be at the barn by seven anyway, so he might as well go early and get Tessa ready. She was going back to the farm when they dropped Rat off. And he should get Rat's stall ready.

Rat was going to be his. He'd told Frank to stop looking for another groom. Frank had known that the decision had been Rob's, not Dad's, but he hadn't been having much luck finding anyone willing to care for Rat. Rat's reputation, with Beak's help, was not a good one.

Something smelled awful, which wasn't unusual in these concrete cubicles, but Rob had a feeling he was smelling himself. Looking down, he saw that his T-shirt and jockey shorts were covered with vomit. Hoping he hadn't puked in front of anyone, he peeled off his foul-smelling underwear. He slipped into jeans and, grabbing a towel, headed for the shower.

Another groom was coming out as he went in. "Stay out of stall 7. Some jerk puked all over the floor and the seat," he said.

Scowling, Rob ducked into the shower. Washing quickly, he fled back to his room. No one ever stayed long in the musty, urine-soaked bathroom with its open rows of toilets and communal showers.

He made it to the barn twenty minutes before anyone else. He fed his horses and began to ready Tessa for her trip to the farm. By the time she was brushed and ready, everyone had fed their horses and was leaving for the cafeteria—everyone except Dusty, who gestured for Rob to follow him into Rat's empty stall.

In the stall, Dusty crouched in one corner and lit a joint. "Only way to deal with a hangover, pal," he said, offering Rob a hit.

"Not for me," he said.

"What do you mean, Mr. Goody?" said Dusty. "I saw you last night trading hits on a joint with Dixie."

"Last night was purely social. I don't do dope."

"You drink enough to make up for it, right?"

Already tired of listening to Dusty, Rob walked out of the stall. He had forgotten to put the salve on Tessa's knees. "Well, little girl, you're going to get a rest," he said softly as he entered her stall. He bent over to apply the medicine. Her knees were badly swollen but healing nicely, as was the cut over her eye. She was a little muscle-sore, but no permanent damage seemed to have been done. If he hadn't come back to the track when he did, Tessa would be in a lot worse shape. He hugged her around her neck.

Hearing the rumbling approach of a horse van, he peered out of the stall. He hadn't seen Kylie since Sunday. If he slipped around the back of the shed row and over to the cafeteria, he wouldn't have to face her now. Dusty could help them with Rat and Tessa.

The truck, with Michael and Mary in the cab, pulled up in front of the barn. Kylie wasn't with them. Perversely, he was disappointed.

Mary hopped out of the cab. How much had Kylie told her? She had spotted him, so it was too late for escape. He guessed he'd find out.

"Good morning, Rob," she called, smiling broadly. "I thought I had better come along and take a look at Tessa before Michael got her back to the farm. I want to see if she'll need a paddock by herself or if she's well enough to be turned out with the other fillies."

Mary stepped into the barn and her smile froze on her face. Her nostrils widened as she inhaled, looking quizzically at

Rob. The dope! She smelled the dope! She frowned and brushed by Rob into Tessa's stall. If she thought it was his, she wouldn't stay silent for long. "Dusty," Rob snarled over his shoulder, "get rid of that thing and come out here."

"Rob," Michael called, "will you give me a hand with this ramp?" Rob walked toward the van. "You too, Dusty," Michael added.

Rob saw Dusty sauntering after him, a silly grin on his face. Maybe Mary would see Dusty and know it hadn't been Rob who'd been smoking the pot.

Rob and Dusty helped Michael lower the ramp. When it fell to the ground, Rat jumped to the rear of his stall, his eyes wide, showing a crescent of white at the sides. This was not going to be easy.

"Here, Michael—let me get him," Rob said, taking the lead shank from Michael.

"Better you than me, man," Dusty said, giggling. "Everybody get out of the way. Here comes the Rat." He gave a shrill laugh.

Rob walked slowly up the ramp into the van. As soon as he was within striking distance, Rat, ears flattened against his head and teeth bared, darted his head at Rob, narrowly missing him. But unlike that first day in the paddock, Rob wasn't afraid. He knew enough not to challenge Rat's bluff, but to approach him slowly. "Take it easy, fella," he murmured. Carefully, he slipped his hand under Rat's muzzle and managed to attach the lead shank to his halter.

After removing the crossbar from in front of Rat and unsnapping the chains from his halter, Rob coaxed the horse from the stall. Rat stopped at the top of the ramp. "I know you'd rather go back to the farm, but you can't," Rob whispered. Finally, with Rob's gentle prodding, Rat started down the ramp.

When he came to the middle of the ramp, Rat leapt, dragging Rob with him and scattering Dusty and Michael, who were waiting at the bottom. Rob landed on his feet beside Rat, who was gathering himself under his haunches to bolt. Rob remembered Pap saying, "If it comes to a fight, a horse is a lot stronger than you are. You've got to outsmart him 'cause you sure can't outfight him." Instantly, Rob walked toward the shed row as if nothing had happened. It worked. Rat followed, tossing his head and snorting, but still following Rob all the way into his stall.

"That old horse never came off the van that easy," said Dusty, who was walking behind them, keeping a safe distance from Rat's hind feet. As Rob closed the stall door with Rat safely inside, Dusty whispered, "I'm gonna split to finish my joint. Don't worry—I'll be back to work before the breakfast bunch arrives."

Why couldn't Dusty have hung around and acted goofy so Mary would know he was the one who was high? A trickle of sweat ran down Rob's cheek and he wiped it away, smelling stale beer as his hand passed in front of his nose. Would she be able to smell the beer on him, too? It seemed to be oozing from his pores.

Mary came out of Tessa's stall, leading the filly behind her. "Well, Rob," she said, "I saw you take Rat off the van. It looks like you two are going to get along fine."

"Sure does seem like the old rebel has met his match," said Michael.

"I hope so," Rob said, taking Tessa from Mary and leading her to the van.

After Tessa was loaded and secured inside the van, Michael and Mary climbed into the cab. Mary still hadn't said anything about the pot. "Rob, I want you to remember something about Rat," she said, leaning out of the cab's window. "I know you think you're forging some kind of relationship with him, but I don't want you to count on that too much. Rat's as unpredictable as they come."

Rob knew what she was saying was important, but he was still trying to find a way to explain about Dusty's pot. About the smell of stale beer. About Kylie and Sunday night.

"You're assuming Rat's actually thinking before he acts," she continued. "You might get him so he can be handled in the stall, but when he's out on the racetrack and decides to stick his toes in, he won't even think of you. He'll just react, and believe me, there's no thought involved in that."

Rob wanted to tell her that that was what he had done on Sunday night—just reacted—and would she please tell Kylie he was sorry? But he didn't know if she knew about Sunday night. And maybe she knew the pot had been Dusty's. And maybe she didn't smell the beer on him. So all he answered was, "I know, Mary."

But when she and Michael drove off, he had to fight an impulse to yell for them to stop. Instead, he stood in the middle of the drive watching them go, feeling disconnected.

Rob returned to Rat's stall to find the horse quietly munching hay. He tried to shake the bad vibes that had been circling him all morning. "Come here, Rat," he called, just for something to say, not really expecting Rat to respond. But Rat came to stand within two feet of him. "So you're willing to meet me halfway, huh?" he said, slowly stepping forward. Rat thrust his nose into Rob's stomach, lipping his T-shirt. Rob laughed. "You're looking for carrots, aren't you?" He stroked the horse's head and Rat actually leaned into his hand. "You're not a bad horse, Rat," he murmured. "We'll show them, won't we?"

Rob went about his morning tasks, each one serving to mark off the time until he could jog Rat. But when Rob finally threw the harness up over Rat's back, the horse squealed, and, bringing a hind leg forward, kicked at the straps hanging beside his belly. At the same time, he shot his head around and tried to bite the girth. Fortunately, Rob was out of the way of his feet, and the cross ties kept him from being able to reach the girth or Rob with his teeth. "Now there's no use in fighting this, Rat. I have to jog you," he said. As he slid the crouper under Rat's tail, the horse stomped a hind foot.

The bridle posed the biggest problem. If Rob freed Rat's head from the cross ties to bridle him, the fight would be on. Rat was smart enough to know when he was free and when he wasn't. Rob eased the halter off the horse's nose, slipping it back so that it was secured around his throat. Then he tried to put the bridle on. Without warning, Rat lurched backward. Rob's breath caught at the back of his throat. If Rat threw himself down, the halter could strangle him. With his heart pounding, Rob tried to keep his hands steady as he once again tried to bridle the horse. He eased his fingers into the side of Rat's mouth, exerting pressure to make him open his mouth. Rob slipped the bit into the horse's mouth. This time when Rat lunged forward, Rob slipped the bridle up over his ears.

When Rat calmed, Rob fastened the throatlatch and attached the driving lines, switching the cross ties to the bridle and removing the halter. Done. Well, almost. He still had to hitch him to the cart, and that couldn't be done in the stall. Rat kicked the side of the stall with a loud report.

"Rob, do you think you could use a little help down there?" Frank called.

Rob could hear the tittering giggles of the other grooms up and down the shed row. "No. We're fine." He stroked the horse's neck until he could feel the muscles relaxing under the smooth red hair. Then he led Rat from the stall and fastened him to the cross ties in the aisle. In spite of Rat's trying to kick the jog cart, Rob got him hitched. A kicking strap between the shafts would keep Rat from being able to kick Rob while he was jogging. With great satisfaction, Rob noted the look of surprise on Frank's slack-jawed face. Rob fastened his helmet and he was ready.

As Rob swung into the cart seat, Rat raised his front feet about a foot off the ground in a halfhearted rear. Rob leaned forward in the seat and clucked to the horse, who landed in an easy pace and headed toward the paddock. As Rat came to the paddock gate, he tossed his head and whinnied, loud and shrill. Heads turned in their direction, and Rob sat a little taller as he turned Rat onto the track.

Rat took the bit in his mouth, pulling hard against the lines. Rob felt the power of the horse and knew, if Rat decided to make it a battle, that he wouldn't be able to hold him. No one could. Maybe he'd made a mistake. Maybe he should have let Frank jog Rat. He set his jaw, and, trying to ignore the sudden weakness in his knees, sawed gently on the lines. Rat let up on the bit.

Yeah, he could do it. Rat paced around and around, giving no more trouble than an occasional toss of his head. Rob quickly forgot any edge of fear, remembering it only as a thrill. Now Rat seemed to loom larger than ever in front of him. He was constantly aware of the tremendous power of the horse harnessed to the cart. He could feel it in the lines, see it in the rippling muscles of the horse's hindquarters, and hear it in the sharp tattoo of Rat's iron-clad hooves on the hard dirt of the track.

Rob gave in to the sensations, letting them force all thought from his mind. He was an extension of the animal in front of him, moving when he moved, reacting when he reacted. Rat picked up his pace, though only slightly. The warm summer air now brushed over Rob's face and hair with more insistence. Rob gripped the lines, sensing he would soon have to pull Rat up and go back to the barn. But for now, Rob was strong, Rob was free.

Rob whistled as he mounted the slight rise that led to the cafeteria. He guessed he'd just told Frank how things were going to be. If Frank had ever had any doubts about it, he now knew he wasn't Rob's boss. No one was.

Frank had been posting the Thursday work schedule and had listed Rat to work last, late in the morning when Dad was due back from his trip.

"Frank, I'm going to work Rat this morning," Rob had said.

"I don't know, Rob. I think your father . . . ," Frank had begun.

"Look," Rob snapped, "if Dad's late, then Rat doesn't get a workout, and he has to be worked today if he's going to race on Sunday." Still Frank said nothing. "I take full responsibility for my actions, all right?"

That had done it. Frank, looking relieved, had mumbled, "Then it's no skin off my nose what you do."

That's right, Frank, old pal, thought Rob, throwing open the door to the cafeteria. That was the way things were going to be, and Frank had better get used to it. All he needed now was a little coffee to drive away the morning fuzzies. But the smell of coffee that filled the room played havoc with his stomach. A large burp, tasting of stale beer, fought its way to the surface. Maybe he'd better get his caffeine from the soft-drink machine.

The small room off the cafeteria that held the vending machines was empty, except for a girl bent over the coin release of one of the pop machines. She stood up, falling against the machine. It was Dixie. "Oh Robbie, baby. I can't seem to get this damn machine to work. Be an angel and get me a Coke." She pressed her change into Rob's hand, two dimes and a quarter.

Rather than attempt to explain that the soda cost fifty cents, he reached into his own pocket and added a nickel. He bought Dixie her drink, then got one for himself.

"What happened to you, woman? You weren't this wrecked when I left you last night."

"Well, I know . . ." She looked sheepishly at Rob and then laughed.

"Dixie, Beak came around, didn't he?"

"I know I shouldn't have gone with him, Rob, but . . . oh hell, Beak can be a lot of fun. And he was really sorry about being so scary on Sunday."

"Damn it, Dixie." He had walked her to her room and made sure she'd locked the door so Beak couldn't get to her. How was he going to take care of her if she pulled stunts like that?

"It was all right, Rob. Really. Except that Beak got into an all-night card game at that dive he goes to and I had nothing to do but sit and drink all night. God, I feel awful."

Rob wasn't feeling so great himself, and now his anger was working on his already-churning stomach. "How do you think this makes me feel?" Rob began as the door opened and Kylie walked in. Rob's queasy stomach jumped into his throat. He couldn't breathe and he was afraid he was going to vomit. Kylie smiled nervously. Rob forced the corners of his mouth up, but Kylie frowned as she looked past him at Dixie.

Completely unaware of Kylie and ignoring Rob's last question, Dixie stuffed two red oval pills into her mouth, washing them down with Coke. "There. That'll get me through the morning." She stumbled toward Rob and planted a wet kiss on his lips. "Thanks, lover. You're a real lifesaver." And then she left by the cafeteria door.

Kylie strode toward the steps of the administration offices. Rob stood stupidly by the pop machine. "Kylie?"

She stopped and turned, not really looking at him. "I have to deliver this vaccination certificate to the racing office," she said.

"Oh" was all he said. He hated that look on her face— eyebrows raised, lips pursed, nose in the air. She started again toward the door. "Kylie, I'm going to work Rat today," he blurted, hoping it would make a difference.

"How is he?" she asked.

"He's fine. Good, in fact. I mean . . . we're getting along great, like you said we would."

She smiled and her face softened. "I'm glad, Rob. When are you going to work him?"

"Probably in about an hour."

"I'll be watching. I won't be able to get down to the paddock because we're busy this morning. But I'll watch from the hill, all right?" She looked at him uncertainly before starting up the stairs.

"Hey, maybe I'll see you later then?" he called.

The door swung open behind him, and Dixie sailed through, stuffing a doughnut into her mouth. She slapped him on his hip as she went by. "See you later, sweetie," she crooned as she breezed out the far door.

When Rob turned back to Kylie, she was already climbing the steps. "I don't think so, Rob," she said in her better-than-anyone tone.

To hell with her then. Rob charged out of the room and headed back toward the barn. He didn't need her either. The stuck-up . . .

"Rob Walsh. Call the switchboard," came the announcement over the paging system. "Rob Walsh. Call the switchboard."

He hesitated, downing the rest of his pop. Right beside him was a phone station. Crushing his now empty can in his right hand, he picked up the phone with his left. "Rob Walsh here," he mumbled.

"Just a minute, Rob," answered Betty, the operator. "Your grandfather's on the line."

Oh, crap! Rob thought. Just what he needed.

"Robbie, son, what's going on down there?" boomed Granddad's voice through the receiver.

"Um . . . hello, Granddad. What do you mean?"

"I've been trying to get you on the phone for three days. I thought you'd call on Sunday. When you didn't call by Tuesday, I started to call your father's trailer. Finally, last night, I called that Tillie person who runs the place. She said she hadn't seen you or your father since the weekend. Where have you been?"

"Dad's away for a few days on a buying trip. I've been staying here in the grooms' quarters. Nothing's wrong."

"What? Your father went off and left you alone at the racetrack? That's it, Robbie! I think you'd better come home—now," Granddad bellowed.

Rob could hear the faint but distinguishable voice of his mother now in the background saying, "Dad, what's the matter? Who are you talking to this early?"

"It's Robbie, Fran," answered Granddad. "Yes, he's perfectly all right. Rob, I'm not finished with you yet, but say hello to your mother."

"Robbie, hi," Mom said, brightly. Rob could imagine her standing, probably in the kitchen, running her fingers through her sleep-tousled curls, still dressed in one of her many pastel robes. "How are you doing?"

"Fine, Mom. How about you?"

"I'm terrific. Do you remember that huge country estate I listed out in Old Maplewood? Well, I'm closing on it today. Our commission is fantastic, and furthermore, because of this sale, I may get another listing in . . ."

"That's great, Mom, but I have to get back to work," Rob interrupted.

"Just a minute, dear—your grandfather's trying to tell me something."

Oh, no, thought Rob. Why couldn't they just let him get back to work?

"So Hal's taken off," came his mother's voice once more, but with that harsh edge to it that he hated. "This is so typical."

"Mom, he hasn't taken off. He's just away for a few days. In fact, he's due back this morning."

"Of course you'd stick up for him. You always stick up for him. Well, this wasn't part of the deal I made with him when I permitted him to take you for the summer. But then deals and promises never meant anything to him except where his damned horses were concerned. They came before everything. Apparently, they still do. Just a minute, Rob . . . Yes, Dad, of course I agree."

Rob shifted impatiently from one foot to the other. It was always like this. He could go for days without thinking much about her—leave her in a safe little walled-off room in a dusty corner of his mind. But when she emerged, she could get to him more than anyone—except maybe Dad. Why didn't he just tell her to shut up, that he was staying here with Dad, that he didn't have to listen to her anymore?

"Rob, your grandfather and I think you should come home."

"Well, I'm not coming," Rob said. "Dad needs me here. He's shorthanded and, Mom, you promised I could spend the summer." Instinctively, Rob knew this was no time to push it further.

"Robbie, you're upsetting me," Mom said icily.

He hated this. *Leave me alone*, he pleaded silently. "I don't want to upset you, Mom, but . . ."

"Then you are going to come home? Just a minute, Robbie." He could hear her talking to Granddad. "Yes, Dad, I think he's coming home."

Why did she think she could manipulate him like this? Well, she couldn't. "Mom!" he yelled. "Mom, get back on the phone."

"Don't get smart with me, Rob," his mother snapped.

He planted his feet and squared his shoulders. "Mom, you promised I could spend the summer here," he asserted.

"Well, I guess I did, but I don't know now." She was waffling. Rob knew the signs. "Rob, your grandfather wants to speak to you."

"Your father has behaved in a most irresponsible manner, Rob," Granddad said. "Why, you hadn't been there more than a few days before he went off. What he's done is wrong and . . . uncaring."

Granddad wasn't fighting fair. Rob clenched the receiver

in both hands, the nails on one hand digging into the back of the other. "That's not so. Dad went because he had to go. He didn't do anything wrong. He trusts me, that's all. He knows I can take care of myself."

Dusty ambled past Rob. "Man, you had better lower your voice. I could hear you yellin' all the way across the parking lot."

"Shut the hell up," snarled Rob. "I didn't mean you, Granddad. I was talking to someone here."

"Rob, all we're giving you is a reprieve. I hope you're telling the truth about your father coming back today, because I intend to call him no later than tomorrow to find out what's going on there."

"Granddad, I have to get back to work," Rob pleaded.

"You go on to work. Your mother has gone to get ready for her meeting, but she says good-bye. Now you listen to me— you are to call home on Sunday night. I will be here waiting for your call."

"Okay, I will," Rob said impatiently.

"And Rob . . ."

"Granddad, I have to go," wailed Rob.

"Rob, your father could have taken you with him. I would have."

"Good-bye," Rob said, slamming the phone into the cradle before he even heard his grandfather's farewell. Rob's head was swimming and his nausea violent. He ran to the shrubs at the edge of the parking lot and vomited.

Rob charged down the shed row, his grandfather's words still ringing in his ears—"Your father could have taken you with him." Well, so what? Granddad had a way of getting him all twisted up.

Reaching Rat's stall, he threw open the door and stormed in. Rat whirled, ready to kick. Stupid! Stupid! No matter how angry he was, he had to be calm around Rat. The horse sensed the least tension in anyone. "Sorry, Rat," Rob whispered. Backing out of the stall, Rob threw himself onto the tack trunk.

Dusty shuffled toward him wearing the same T-shirt he'd had on the night before with "Born to Party" in fluorescent letters across his scrawny chest. "What's the matter, Rob old buddy? You're certainly testy this morning."

"None of your damned business, Dusty."

Dusty giggled and shuffled past.

"Why don't you try getting some work done, jerk?" Rob yelled after him.

"Look who's playing the boss's son all of a sudden," he said, continuing down the aisle.

Jerks, all of them. Rob was still too worked up to risk handling Rat. He'd jog Sam first.

Out on the track with Sam, he felt better. The track wasn't too crowded yet; that was how Rob liked it best. The grandstand was empty except for a few maintenance men, who were sweeping the stands and box seats. In the center field, a gardener weeded the flower-filled medallion that displayed Farmington's stylized *F.P.* logo in yellow and orange marigolds. Rob threw his head back and let the sun warm his face. Mom and Granddad were far from here. They couldn't get to him now.

Around the track he went at an easy swinging trot, letting the even rhythms of Sam's hooves on the hard earth soothe him. By the time the jog was finished, he was relaxed enough to face Rat.

As he stood in front of Rat's stall, taking his harness from its vinyl bag, Rob noticed everyone else in the barn slowed the pace of their work to watch him. Hadn't the past two days shown them he could handle Rat? Rat had hardly fussed at all yesterday when Rob had harnessed and then jogged him.

Rob caught Frank watching as he went into Rat's stall. Rat turned to face Rob. "Easy now, Rat. You don't want to make a fool out of me, do you?" Rob whispered. Rat blew several short puffs of air from his nostrils and stomped a front foot, but let Rob fasten the cross ties to his halter. Rob ran his hands down Rat's neck. Moving slowly, he circled the horse's neck with his arms and laid his cheek against the warm, firm flesh. Rob didn't hold him long, but for the moment he did, he was sure he felt the muscles in the horse's neck relax.

And although he couldn't be sure, he thought Rat had leaned into him.

Feeling warm and full and right, Rob harnessed and hitched the stallion, who stood quietly, allowing it. Rob fastened his helmet and made sure he had his stopwatch. The overcheck still hung loose from the crown of the bridle, and Rob reached to hook the other end to the top of the belly band. Rat pawed the gravel drive impatiently. As Rob moved around to the cart seat, Rat shook his head loose and charged off toward the track. With a run and a leap Rob landed, laughing, in the cart seat. After all, he'd never wanted Rat to lose all of his fire.

Rob struggled to keep Rat at an easy pace for the first few warm-up trips. After much head tossing and a few bucks, Rat settled.

As they came toward the paddock on their last trip, Rob saw Frank, Jan, and Dusty standing outside of the barn on the rise, watching him. He looked back over his shoulder toward Barn Fifteen. The lone figure on the hill was Kylie. Good.

"All right, Rat," he said, turning the horse before the grandstand to begin the pace to the starting pole. "Let's show them what we can do." Rat tossed his head and reared. Involuntarily, Rob drew back the long training whip, hoping a cut on the neck might bring him back down onto all four feet. No, with this horse that would be the wrong move. Rob leaned forward and clucked, slapping the lines gently on Rat's sides. Rat lunged forward, almost pulling the left line from Rob's hand. Grateful that he had thought to fasten his helmet before mounting the cart, Rob sawed gently but firmly on the lines to bring the horse back under control. Rat submitted until the starting line was in front of him and, then, without waiting for Rob to cue him, took off. The force snapped Rob's head back. Recovering, he again sawed on the lines. Rat wasn't supposed to be worked fast today, not after being turned out.

But the big horse was bearing down on the starting line like a freight train on open track, completely ignoring Rob's signals. Rob had not thought to ask Frank how fast the horse should be worked, but knew he shouldn't be going this fast.

Rat pulled himself around a slower-moving horse as they flashed by the starting pole. Remembering the group watching from the barn, Rob stopped working the lines. It wasn't helping anyway, and at least he could sit there pretending he was in control. Rat felt the change and took a firmer hold on the bit. Rob's arms felt like they were being pulled from their sockets. Yet he couldn't give up entirely and let the horse have his own head. He had to stay calm. Rat wasn't crazy. If Rob just sat tight, he'd be fine.

Around the upper turn they flew and on past the grandstand. The concussion of Rat's hooves, digging into the track, bore into Rob's brain. Never had he driven a horse with this kind of speed. They seemed to be flying. Slower horses along the rail pulled aside to let them pass as Rat charged up behind them. Rob glanced at his stopwatch. He'd forgotten to start it.

Again they were coming to the starting line, and Rat went on without showing any sign of slowing. Rob's nervousness gave way to a cold, clutching fear. Sweat began to pour from under his helmet. The mile was almost finished. Would he be able to stop Rat? Testing, he worked the lines. Rat only surged forward, clenching the bit more tightly in his teeth. He wouldn't be able to stop unless Rat decided he wanted to. Rob's knees, bent in the stirrups, trembled.

As they rounded the upper turn, Rat once more seemed to

pick up speed. How could that be? When they swung into the stretch, with the finish line in sight, Rob knew he was right—Rat was now pacing faster than Rob could have imagined possible. Exhilaration mixed with fear until he was giddy. This was incredible! He imagined the grandstand was full and spectators crowded the apron. He and Rat led a whole field of pacers down the stretch and across the finish line to win by three lengths. The crowd roared its approval.

Then Rat slowed. As if he had raced a real race, Rat was pulling himself up. So the old Rat wasn't going to make him look bad after all. The hands Rob had kept steady during the drive now began to shake. When they came to the paddock, Rob went through the motions as if he were pulling Rat up. He forced his hands to hold firm. He went past the paddock, glancing at the rise by the barn. Four now watched, although he couldn't make out who they were.

Farther up the backstretch, Rat allowed himself to be turned, and, with his best manners, walked through the paddock and up to the barn. Then Rob recognized the fourth person. Dad was back. With clenched jaws Dad stormed at Rob and Rat. The grooms slunk into the shadows of the shed row, pretending to have been about their business all along.

"Hi, Dad," Rob said with forced cheerfulness as he dismounted the cart.

"What in the hell do you think you're doing?" Dad shouted. "You had no business going a training mile without my permission. Going that fast with a horse that's been turned out is insane!" Rob had never seen Dad this mad—at least not at him. "Of course, you don't know, because you didn't even think to take your stopwatch, did you?" Rob, beginning to get angry himself, looked away. "Well, Frank clocked it. You just went a training mile in 1:59 flat."

Rob had never dreamed they had gone that fast. Rat could have gotten hurt. Exploding into his memory came Mom's accusation that the horses were all Dad really cared about. Rob began to strip Rat, who was dripping with sweat and blowing heavily. "All you care about are these damned horses," Rob mumbled.

"What did you say?" Dad demanded.

"I said that Mom was right—all you care about is your damned horses!"

"If that's all you've got to say for yourself, it's not going to cut it with me," Dad roared.

"I couldn't help it, all right?" Rob shouted back. Rat shied to the side, pulling Rob with him. "Easy, fella," soothed Rob, patting the horse's neck. When Rat again relaxed, Rob continued more softly. "Look, he took off with me. I would never hurt him on purpose, and if you don't know that by now, I quit." Rob ran his hands down Rat's front legs, checking for any sign of swelling that would indicate a strain. When he looked up again, Dad was trying not to laugh.

The laugh burst from deep in his chest. "I should have suspected that. He did it with me once. Only then he went in 1:59.3." Rob smiled in spite of the anger that still flickered. "You still shouldn't have driven him without me here, but under the circumstances, you did a good job of controlling him." Dad threw an arm around Rob's shoulder. "I'll bet that scared the pants off you. It did me when I was in the driver's seat." Dad then reached up to brush the forelock out of Rat's eyes. The horse dove at him.

"He doesn't like to have his forelock touched, Dad," said Rob flatly.

"You think you know him pretty well, don't you?"

"Yeah, I do," Rob said.

"Well, you may know him, or at least get along with him better than the rest of us, but I've got to warn you: Never assume you can predict what he's going to do. As soon as you get careless, he's going to get you. I should take you off him for that stunt you just pulled, and also because I consider him dangerous." Dad watched as Rob stroked Rat's sweat-drenched neck. "But you really do seem to get along with him, and to be honest with you, I've never had a groom on him who did. That might make all the difference with this horse."

"Does that mean I stay on him?"

"For now, it does," Dad said, studying Rat. "But if I see you getting careless around him, you're done. Your mother would have a fit if anything happened to you, and then she'd probably never let you stay with me again."

Rob finished stripping the last of the harness from Rat's hot back. Why was it that even when Dad was giving him what he wanted, Dad's answers never quite seemed to satisfy him? Dad fell into step with him as he walked Rat toward the wash area. He didn't want trouble with Dad. At least Dad never bossed him around like Mom and Granddad did. "Hey, Dad," Rob said, trying to muster a feeling of closeness with him, "how many horses did you buy for us?"

"I bought three. But what do you mean 'for us,' smart mouth?"

"I guess that depends on you, Dad. But you should know I wasn't as afraid out there as you think. I kind of liked it. Bet I make a great driver."

"I've always thought you would. And if you're telling me you think your old man needs a partner, I'd say you'd make a good one," Dad said, looking hard at Rob.

"I guess that's what I'm saying," Rob answered.

Dad's eyes looked misty. "Son, you know this is what I've always wanted."

Rob ran a wet sponge over Rat's back. "Me, too, Dad," he mumbled. Even if it wasn't working out quite the way he'd dreamed, it did seem to answer the problems of the moment. Then why was a case of the spooks creeping up on him again? He wasn't alone in an empty house or trailer. He was outside on a balmy June morning. And Dad was back.

14

As Rob led Rat toward the paddock, the horse tossed his head, his mane leaping from his neck like tongues of flame. It had been four weeks and three races since Rat had been brought from the farm. Was it time to turn him out again?

When they came to the paddock gate Rat reared, tearing the lines from Rob's hand. Rob quickly recovered the lines, but still Rat refused to enter the paddock. "Take it easy, now. You're not some skittish colt who's never raced before," Rob said. But Rat continued to fuss.

The security guard on the paddock gate shook his head. "You don't need to tell me who that one is, Rob—Nobel's Stoutheart, for the fourth race," he said, checking them off on his entry sheet.

A groom, leading a horse behind them, shouted, "Get him through the gate or take him back to the barn."

Rob tugged on the lines; after some more head tossing, Rat moved through the gate. Dad waited by the entrance to the track, waving him on.

"He's getting goofy on us again, isn't he?" Dad asked irritably.

"Not too bad," Rob answered. Again Rat tried to rear as Rob fastened the overcheck.

"He's probably due to be turned out. This is as long as he's ever gone," Dad said, mounting the bike. With no more protest from Rat except another toss of his head and a halfhearted, one-legged kick, Dad drove Rat onto the track for the first lap of his first warm-up trip. Rob watched them go. Rat had been racing great. He'd won his last three starts, leading from wire to wire.

"Hey, cutie, over here," Dixie called, leaning over the chain-link fence that separated the paddock from the walkway to the grandstand.

"You've got it?" asked Rob, walking over to her.

"All on the nose, right?"

"We better play it across the board tonight. The old Rat's a bit ornery."

"I'll be back at the barn right after the ninth race with our winnings," she said, walking away and patting the hip pocket of her jeans to let Rob know where she was carrying his money.

Dixie had been carrying Rob's bets since he had decided to plunk Granddad's hundred dollars down on a win ticket in Rat's first race. Dad had felt it was a pretty safe bet. Rat almost always won his first start after being turned out. Since the charts in the program were based on his last starts—the bad ones before he'd been sent to the farm—the odds were high. Rob was six hundred dollars richer after Rat's first race.

The odds had been less the past two weeks, but Rob had

nearly one thousand dollars in a bank account in town. He figured if he watched the way Rat behaved and was careful with his wagers, Rat would buy him his first car.

He'd made it a good deal for Dixie, too, paying her 5 percent on all profits for carrying his bets. He could trust her not to cheat him, and she was sober enough early in the evening to remember what she was doing. Besides, he almost always wrote everything down for her.

Rob went back to the race stall to check Rat's equipment and draw a bucket of water for him. When he returned to the rail, he saw Dad and Rat coming toward him around the lower clubhouse turn. Man, did they look good—Rat big and brilliantly red under the lights, his pace quick and powerful; Dad so handsome in his crisp red-and-white satin colors. If only he could predict what Rat would do tonight. Rat was the fastest horse in the race, but speed was never the only factor with him.

A driver dismounted a cart as a groom gathered the horse in front of Rob. Rob recognized Whimsy Pinehill, the gelding who had finished second to Rat in the past three starts. Dad said you could never discount Whimsy Pinehill, but Rob didn't consider him much of a threat. Rat had a record of 1:57.2; Whimsy Pinehill's was only 2:00.4. The gelding even looked like a tired hack horse. As soon as his groom unfastened the overcheck, the brown gelding dropped his jugged head and walked slowly away. This horse showed no fire, no spirit. Still, he was steady, like Sam's Option.

Rob took a racing program from his pocket and turned to the fourth race. Whimsy Pinehill's record showed twenty starts this year, with twelve wins, six seconds, and two thirds—as well as earnings of over eighty thousand dollars.

Rat had only started twelve times, with five wins, one second, and six also-rans; he hadn't even earned thirty thousand dollars yet.

Dad turned Rat and headed back to the paddock with him. Rat shook his head, fighting the overcheck. Rob studied the breadth of Rat's chest; his long, powerful legs; and his bright, intelligent eye. Whimsy Pinehill would find out again tonight that "slow and steady" didn't always win the race.

Together, he and Dad got Rat into his race stall, and then Dad was off to warm up another horse. Rob kept looking at the plain, brown head of Whimsy Pinehill in the stall next to Rat's. The horse looked half asleep. Up and down the whole shed row, horses tossed their heads, nipped at their grooms, and pawed the gravel in front of their stalls—Rat more than all of them. Grooms bustled in and out of stalls—wrapping legs, fastening loose straps, adjusting cross ties—caught, like their horses, in the excitement of race night. Whimsy Pinehill's groom, having already cared for his charge, sat on an overturned bucket in front of the stall.

When the grooms led the horses into place for the post parade, Whimsy Pinehill showed his first signs of spirit. Rat had leapt onto the track, nearly knocking Rob down, and Whimsy Pinehill calmly walked by. As his groom attached the overcheck and his driver swung into the seat, the gelding's head came up and his ears pricked forward. He broke into a jaunty pace, giving a short, rumbling nicker that ended in a whinny. His groom stepped up beside Rob. "I never took care of one that loved to race more than he does," he commented.

Rob watched the brown horse slow as he came to Rat, who was acting up, giving a few stiff-legged hops. It wouldn't matter how much Whimsy Pinehill loved to race; Rat was faster. Quickly Rat settled into a steady pace, taking his position in the post parade.

As they came in front of the grandstand, Rob saw the crowd on the apron surge forward for a look at their favorites. The murmur from the grandstand floated toward him across the center field, bringing with it the smell of popcorn, hot dogs, and hot sausage from the many food stands. The announcer called the horses by name as they paraded in front of the grandstand.

At the top of the stretch, the horses turned for their final score, falling into place behind the mobile starting gate. As they came toward the paddock, Rob saw Rat toss his head as if he was about to break stride and go into a gallop. "Come on, Rat, stay flat—no breaks tonight," he whispered. Next to Rat, Whimsy Pinehill paced steadily toward the starting line. Rob glanced at the televised projection of the tote board. Rat was the favorite, with odds of 4:5.

As the field reached the starting line and the gate swung away, Rat burst into a gallop. Dad immediately pulled him back on the pace, but they were now at the back of the field. Dad pulled Rat to the outside and in no time they were on the move. By the time they reached the top of the grandstand, Rat had caught the leaders, pacing third on the outside next to Whimsy Pinehill, who was second; the number five horse led the field. They sailed by the grandstand locked in position, the crowd urging them on.

As the horses headed toward the paddock, the grooms began a rumbling of their own: "Attaboy, stay right there" . . . "Easy now, big fella" . . . "Mine's sittin' pretty." Rob watched silently as Rat charged toward him on the outside, the bright lights playing golden along the crest of his neck. Rat was flying. Rob held his breath.

Right in front of the paddock, Rat broke into a rolling, high-legged gallop. Rob and the crowd in the grandstand groaned together. This time Rat fought Dad's efforts to get him back on stride and was three lengths behind the field before he was pacing again.

Up the backstretch they raced, with Rat quickly gaining on the field. At the top of the final stretch, Whimsy Pinehill made his move, easily passing the now-tired lead horse. He took the lead by two lengths. But Rat was moving up on the outside. He charged into second, catching Whimsy Pinehill in four strides. Dad pulled Rat alongside the leader and they flew toward the finish line. "All right, Rat! Do it!" yelled Rob, jumping in the air.

Rat passed first the hips and then the flank and then the nose of the brown gelding. The finish line was right in front of them. The roar of the crowd swelled, seeming to carry the big red horse forward. Rat took the lead by half a length. Then, suddenly, he broke into a gallop and ran, not paced, across the finish line.

"Oh, Rat, no," Rob groaned. An angry buzz came from the grandstand. Cheers soon followed for the rest of the field.

On the televised tote board, Rat's number three and Whimsy Pinehill's number four began to flash wildly, indicating the need for a judges' decision. Rob stepped forward to take Rat from Dad, who was heading back to the paddock. Dad, like Rob, already knew what the judges would decide.

As Dad dismounted, Rat tossed his head, fighting the overcheck. "Wait a minute, Rat," Rob said, "I'm trying to free it."

"Get this damned nag cooled out; I'll be up after the eighth race. We're going to have a talk," Dad said with anger in his voice. He stomped off toward the locker room without even looking at Rob.

"Don't bother," muttered Rob. He was sick of being treated like a groom instead of a son. All day long they worked, he and Dad. All evening Dad raced. Then after the races Dad hustled around, sucking up to his owners or chasing Nicole. There'd been no sessions on the track to prepare Rob for his license. There were no invitations to join Dad after the races. Well, if he could get Rat cooled out before Dad returned, Dad wouldn't be able to find him for that "talk."

Glancing over his shoulder, Rob saw Whimsy Pinehill calmly circling in the backstretch, waiting for the development of the finish-line photograph from which the judges would make their decision. His driver, too, knew what it would be. Rob was halfway to the barn when the announcement came: "Because of a lapped-on break at the wire, the number three horse, Noble's Stoutheart, is moved to second place and the number four horse, Whimsy Pinehill, is the winner of the fourth race."

Rat jumped sideways and nearly stepped on Rob's foot. "Cut it out, Rat," said Rob. "You've caused enough trouble for one evening." Rob certainly wouldn't make much money from his bets tonight.

Rob had Rat nearly cooled off, walking him around and around the gravel drive that circled the barn, before the horse's nervous energy quelled. Rob had been stepped on, nearly bitten, and frequently bumped as he'd unharnessed, then bathed, then walked the stallion. Fortunately, he'd long ago given up wearing tennis shoes around Rat. He needed the greater protection of leather boots.

The eighth race was over by the time Rat was cool enough

to put in his stall. Dad had won it with a colt of Frank's, but Rob wasn't counting on him being in a better mood. It was time to disappear. He'd slip back later to meet Dixie. Quickly, he pulled the red-and-white blanket off Rat. He ran his hands once more over the fiery red hair of the horse's back and then again under his belly. Rat was completely cooled, fussing to be freed. "All right, Rat. I'm anxious to be out of here, too," Rob snapped, jerking the lead shank free of the horse's halter.

Rat shied away from the flapping leather end of the shank. Rob dove for the opened bottom of the stall door as Rat's hind hooves narrowly missed catching him in the back. The stallion whirled toward Rob. Open-mouthed, Rat snaked his head at him. Rob slammed the stall door. Rat had meant it this time. If Dad hadn't attached that metal grate to the top half of the stall, and if Rob hadn't made a practice of always latching it when he went into the stall . . . Rob threw himself down on the tack trunk, trying to catch his breath. That had been too close.

"Well?" Dad boomed as he stormed around the corner of the barn.

Startled, Rob nearly fell off the trunk. "Well, what?" he said irritably.

"Do you think you can get me one more start out of him before he has to go back to the farm?" Dad demanded.

"Me? What do you mean, can *I* get one more start out of him?"

"I'm just asking for your opinion. You're the one who claims to know him so well."

"Yeah, I do, and you know damn well he's raced better with me taking care of him than he ever has, so what's your problem?"

"It's damned frustrating to know you're sitting on such speed and to have him go nuts on you."

"Well, that's not my fault."

"I know it's not, but that preferred pace next week has a big purse—thirty thousand dollars. As sour as Rat was tonight, I don't imagine he'll win it, but with that kind of money even a third place isn't anything to sneeze at. Do you think you can hold him together until after that race?"

Rob glared at Dad, who looked away from him into Rat's stall. Rat was peacefully nibbling on some hay, with no sign he'd just gone berserk and run Rob out of the stall. Rob had been kind of rough with him, but Rat knew him now and trusted him. He hadn't done anything like that for weeks. He probably did need to be turned out.

"Well, can you hold him together?" Dad challenged.

"One more start should be all right," Rob answered grudgingly. "But I think we should only jog him until then—no training miles. We can add some extra distance jogging to keep him in shape."

Dad grinned. "Not a bad idea, Rob. You're getting to be a pretty sharp horseman."

"You're damned right I am. So what about my license?" Rob glared at him.

"What do you mean? We applied for it; it hasn't come in yet." Dad looked puzzled.

"I know that, but I'm supposed to go to the fairs the end of this month. I have to get those fair drives in, and if you don't work with me, I won't be ready."

"Is that all you're worried about?" Dad said, ruffling Rob's hair and smiling. "So you don't make the July fairs. We'll still have all of August."

Dad could save his forced charm—it wasn't working. Rob looked away. Beyond the shed row Nicole Barrone perched in the passenger seat of the blue T-bird.

"Listen, Rob," said Dad, "I have some plans for this evening. Do you think you could close up the barn for me tonight?" Dad winked and clapped Rob on the shoulder.

"Who in the hell do you think's done it every night for the past two weeks?" Rob snapped. It had also been two weeks since he had slept anywhere but in the grooms' quarters. And he was sick of lying to Granddad when he called and questioned why he could never reach Rob at the trailer.

"You don't really mind, do you? I mean, I thought that since you'd been staying here you wanted . . ."

"What do you know about what I want?"

"Jeez, Rob. I didn't realize . . . I mean, I really thought this was what you wanted. When I was your age, I hated having my old man hanging around all the time." Dad shifted from one foot to the other, looking toward the car to where Nicole waited. "We'll have a talk tomorrow, okay? How about lunch?"

Always a comeback, an attempt to please. Rob sighed. "Don't worry about it. I'll close the barn. I have to wait for Dixie, anyway."

Dad started to walk away, but stopped. Turning back to Rob, he said, "Rob, you're not sleeping with Dixie, are you? Not that it's any of my business or anything, but you should be care . . ."

"You're right," Rob snarled. "It's none of your damned business—but, no, I'm not."

"Well, if you're not, you're the only one who isn't. At one time or another she's been with every man on this racetrack, which is why I want you to be careful." Dad gave a laugh that was both cruel and knowing. Was Dad including himself in that survey? Rob's stomach went sour. "You know what they say, kid—'the difference between love and herpes is that herpes is forever.'" Dad laughed at his joke. "See you tomorrow. Remember, we'll go out for lunch. Someplace nice." Dad walked toward the car.

"You bastard," Rob growled under his breath. "You lousy, stinking bastard."

Rob paced the gravel drive in front of the barn. Dixie was late. The races had been over for at least half an hour. All the horses had been cared for, the other grooms had long gone, the barn had been closed. He looked down on the paddock and over to the grandstand. The grandstand was nearly empty and the paddock lights were off, except for a pale-yellow glow from the lab window.

A truck that looked like Mary's drove out of the paddock parking lot. Probably Mary, Michael, and Kylie. He didn't see them much anymore, but knew they came to see Rat race. He remembered telling Kylie how at night the track seemed so peaceful, so special. The lights went off in the barn across the road. Tonight it just seemed dark.

Nervously Rob scanned the path that led around the lower turn of the track. A lone figure made its way toward the paddock. Dixie? As she passed under one of the huge light poles shining into the valley on the dispersing traffic, the reflected light fell on her. Rob started down the hill at a run.

They met in the shadows by the paddock gate.

"Oh, Rob, we didn't do so good tonight," Dixie said, staggering toward him. She held up her hands, a six-pack in each. "We can drown our sorrows."

Laughing, Rob took one from her. Together they climbed the hill, Rob slowing to keep pace with Dixie, who was already bombed. "Who cares about money? Let's polish these off and forget the whole damned evening," Rob said.

"I hope I can forget it fast enough," Dixie said as they came into the barn.

Rob saw for the first time her badly swollen and cut lip. "What happened?" he asked, grabbing her shoulders and spinning her toward him.

"It's nothing. Don't worry about it." She drew a tissue from her jeans pocket and nervously patted her lip. "It isn't even bleeding anymore."

"Beak hit you, didn't he?" demanded Rob.

"Well, yes, but he really didn't mean it. I just didn't pull back fast enough." Dixie forced a laugh. "I think he was as surprised as I was when he connected. I mean, he's always swinging at me, but I always duck."

"Dix, you shouldn't put up with that crap." Poor old Dixie— she was so defenseless. How could anyone . . . The picture of his father and his knowing remarks floated back to Rob. Yeah, how could anyone . . . ?

"Oh, Walsh, suck on a beer and leave me alone." Dixie plopped onto a bale of hay in the feed stall, tossing a beer at Rob.

Rob caught the beer and, opening the can, walked into the stall to sit near her. "But, Dixie, why . . . ?"

"Look, Rob, he was drunk and mean. It's not like he's always batting me around. He was having a bad night. I told him I wasn't up to sitting around watching him play cards all night—that I was going to have a few beers with you and turn in early."

"You told him you were coming here?" Rob asked.

"Don't worry about him. That bartender friend of his pulled him off me and got him out of there. They'll be gone all night playing cards and getting wrecked."

"I'll only drop it if you're sure you're all right."

Dixie threw her arms wide, beer sloshing from the can. "So look at me! I'm fine."

Rob relaxed against the bales of hay and took a deep drink of his beer. The cold liquid ran down his throat, making him feel better. Dixie could take care of herself. But could she? He looked over at her and saw by her heavy eyelids that she wasn't far from sleep. "Hey, Dixie—wake up." Dixie was startled into a more erect posture. She gave him a silly grin before falling back against the wall, her eyes closed. Watching her sleep, he went to work on his six-pack.

After three beers and a quick trip to the toilets in the administration building, Rob sat on the tack trunk outside the stall, looking over the track entrance. A car was coming up the hill fast—far faster than it should have been in the barn area. When it careened toward their barn without slowing, Rob knew who was driving it. By the time it slid to a gravel-spraying stop in front of the barn, Rob was on his feet ready to face Beak. He gave Dixie a glance over his shoulder. She was still sleeping. Rob stepped out to meet Beak as he threw open the car door and stumbled out.

"Where's Dixie? I want Dixie!"

"She's not here. Beat it, Beak," Rob said, amazed he could speak at all with his throat so tight. He wasn't too steady on his feet, but Beak didn't know that.

"He's right, Beak. You get out of here!" Dixie stood in the stall doorway, straw hanging from her limp hair, her clothes rumpled.

"Walsh, you lying scum," Beak yelled, charging him. Caught off guard, Rob was thrown against the side of the barn and took the first punch on his left cheek. The blow drove the back of his head into the barn wall. Despite the pain radiating from his head, Rob pushed himself toward Beak, his fists raised. The edges of his vision had gone fuzzy, but he was able to focus on Beak in the center of the blur. Rob began to punch at Beak's face. Beak came to meet him. But Rob didn't feel flesh against his fists. It seemed that every time he punched at Beak, his own face, chest, or stomach took the blow. The fuzz became a haze. He heard Dixie screaming as he fell to the gravel. *No, not Dixie! Leave her alone!* But he was still taking the blows and they were sharper and harder, no longer flesh hitting flesh. They struck his shoulder, his hip, his thigh. Curling into a fetal position, he threw his hands over his head. But still the blows came.

Suddenly they stopped. Again, Rob heard the sound of wheels screeching to a stop, and now footsteps running away from the barn. He tried to see what was happening, but all was dark. Something hot and sticky covered his face.

Arms circled him and he lay back into them. "Rob! Rob!" Dixie? A car door slammed. Something wiped his eyes. He could see again. Dixie's shirt was covered with blood. No! She wiped his eyes with her shirttail. The blood was his? "Dr. Tanner—it's Rob!" Mary? What was Mary doing there? He looked up from where he lay on the gravel, Dixie's arms around him. Two women stood above him. Kylie? *Please, not Kylie.* Not with him here, like this.

The women knelt and he focused on them. No, Mary was alone. Rob tried to raise himself on his elbow, but fell back onto Dixie.

"Let me see your forehead," Mary said. He could feel her hands, hard and cool, against his cheeks, but the rest of his body burned and throbbed. "It's going to need a few stitches." Rob tried to nod, but pain blazed through his head, a black haze filmed his eyes. He could hear the mumbled conversation of Mary and Dixie, but not what they were saying. He could feel Mary's strong, capable hands feeling his limbs and manipulating his joints. He didn't have to worry. She would take care of him now.

"Rob. Rob, listen to me," Mary's voice was insistent. Rob opened his eyes. He could see her face clearly. He tried to smile. "Rob, do you think you can walk?"

"Yeah," he mumbled, and tried to crawl to his feet. He could feel Dixie's limp hand on his right arm as Mary partially lifted him to his feet. He tried again to smile at Dixie as he leaned away from her into Mary. Dixie couldn't do anything for him, but he wanted her to know that was all right.

Somehow, either by his own power or Mary's, he crawled into the cab of the truck. Where was she taking him? To the farm, of course. And he could stay there with her and Michael and Kylie. Rob drifted off into his dreams.

The stopping of the truck jarred him awake. They were at the hospital. What were they doing there? He was all right. Stitches. Mary had said something about stitches.

But parental consent was needed for treatment and, though Mary phoned all the likely places, Dad was not to be found. Finally, Mary spotted an old friend—a doctor, who reluctantly agreed to examine Rob.

It was a long time before the doctor was finished with him.

He was poked, prodded, X-rayed, and stitched. Mary bustled in and out, questioning the nurses, the technicians, and even the doctor. Finally, Rob was pronounced well enough to leave, with nothing more seriously wrong than severe bruises and the cut over his left eye that had taken six stitches to close. Then why did he feel so bad? Why was every breath an agony? Bruises, just bruises. But Rob's biggest ache was deeper than the bruises, deeper even than Beak's boots had reached. Where was Dad? Mom? Mary had her arms around him, helping him into the cab of her truck, but those weren't the arms he needed.

"It's all right, Rob," Mary said. "I'm taking you to the trailer and I'll wait with you until your father comes home."

As they pulled up to the trailer, Rob could see by the T-bird parked in front that Dad was home. He sure hoped they weren't walking in on anything. But so what if they were? He was hurt. He needed Dad.

Mary told him to wait in the truck. Was she leery, too, of walking in on Dad and Nicole, or was she trying to protect him from it? Mary knocked on the door, which was opened almost immediately by Dad. "Hey, Mary, what are you doing here? Nicky took me out to try sushi. We're having a nightcap. Come on in. Nicky," he called over his shoulder, "get Mary a beer."

"The party's over, Hal. I've brought Rob home—Beak worked him over," Mary said.

Dad disappeared momentarily into the trailer, but soon was at Rob's side. "Oh, no, Robbie," he said, peering into the cab.

Tears started to come and Rob banished them. Dad put his arms around him from one side and Mary from the other, supporting him as he limped into the house. He heard the sound of Nicole's car driving away as he mounted the steps.

At least he wouldn't have to put up with her. Dad and Mary took him straight back to his bed and laid him on it.

"Now, Rob, tell me what happened." Dad, too, was trying not to cry.

"Hal, don't make him talk. I'll tell you what I know and you can get the rest from Rob in the morning. While you get him undressed, I'll get an ice bag for his head."

The sheets felt cool and smooth against Rob's bruised body; the pillow was a soft refuge for his aching head. Mary came in and carefully placed the ice bag on his forehead. Softly, she kissed his cheek before leaving him alone again with Dad.

"We'll get that son of a bitch, Rob," Dad said. "I'll file a complaint first thing in the morning."

Rob rolled toward the wall. That wasn't what he needed to hear. Rob waited for Dad to say more, but the silence grew. Finally, he heard his father stand, pushing back the chair he'd pulled up to the bed.

"Well, you try to get some sleep. I know you must be worn out," he said. Rob rolled back toward Dad. Bending over, Dad kissed the top of Rob's head. "I'm so sorry, son," he mumbled, his voice sounding choked.

Dad left the room, but Rob was unable to sleep. Mary's angry voice came to him through the darkness. "For God's sake, Hal, from what I hear, he's bombed every night. He's hanging out with Dusty and Dixie. They party behind Barn Five. Kylie heard about it and she told me yesterday. I was just waiting for a chance to tell you."

Rob forced his head deeper into the pillow.

"Look, Mary, it's none . . ."

"Don't you dare tell me it's none of my business," Mary snapped. "You have always been as close to me as a brother. I love you and Rob. That makes it my business."

The pain in Rob's head lessened, but his stomach contracted.

"I love him, too, Mary, and he knows it. Haven't you heard? He's coming into the business with me." Rob could picture Dad grinning broadly, oozing charm—anything to take the heat off.

"Oh, how wonderful," Mary said. "Just like you and your dad. And it's made you so happy."

"What in the hell do you know about it? I am happy."

No, he wasn't, Rob realized, surprised. He really wasn't.

"You're a real picture of happiness, Hal. Every year you drink a little more. And why is it that the girls you chase keep getting younger and younger? When they're that young, they don't expect much from you, do they? They're just impressed with the fact you're a driver, and you've let that be good enough for you."

Rob heard a sob. Dad? Now Rob wished he could sleep.

"Don't do to Rob what your dad did to you," Mary said gently.

"What are you talking about? I always wanted to go into the horse business."

"Come on, Hal. I was your best pal then. You wanted to be a teacher, a gym teacher and baseball coach. Remember? But your dad wanted you to go into the business and it was easier to do what he wanted than to stand up to him."

"I was a hell of a ball player in high school, wasn't I?" Dad asked.

"The best hitter on the team."

"You know, I haven't been to a ball game in years," Dad said, his voice cracking.

Rob tossed the ice bag onto the floor and covered his head with the pillow. "Mary, please leave him alone," he whispered through swollen lips into the mattress. Rob couldn't stand to hear more, but the pillow made his head throb. He tossed the pillow off.

". . . but Rob's caught between Fran and her dad and their plans for him, and you and this stable. You all have him so confused that he hasn't even thought about making any plans for himself," Mary said. Rob heard the outside door open. "Call me in the morning, Hal, if you need anything." The door closed and Rob heard no more.

Memories of his parents' fights from years ago flooded back. How they used to frighten him, the sounds of his parents' angry voices filling every corner of the trailer. His anger began to rise. They should have known he could hear them and that he was too young to be anything but scared. How could a little kid understand such terrible shouting and screaming?

Rob was still angry when he heard his father come back into the trailer and Mary's truck drive away. When Dad entered his room, Rob pretended to sleep. Even when Dad sat on a chair close to the bed, Rob faked the deep, even sighs of sleep. Then Rob heard him. Dad was crying. He tried to block out the sound. He willed sleep to come, but it wouldn't, though his body was leaden and begged for it. *No, Dad*, he thought, *I won't deal with your sadness. Tonight I need you to take care of me.* It seemed like all of his life he'd been dealing with his parents' problems. Well, Dad could cry all night if he wanted to. Rob clenched his teeth in spite of the pain it caused his jaw and tried to think of something else— anything but his father sitting there blubbering like a baby. But nothing could stop the sound of his father's crying.

"Dad, are you all right?" Rob asked.

"I don't know, Rob. I just feel so damned bad."

"Don't cry, Dad. Everything will be okay," Rob soothed,

while part of him argued that this was not the way it was supposed to be. Maybe it was time to quit worrying about what should be. Rob reached out and took his father's hand.

So, with his father's hand held securely in his own, Rob comforted Dad until sleep finally came to free him.

16

"Come on in, Kylie." Dad's voice floated in to Rob. "Rob's still sleeping."

Rob's eyes flew open. He was not still sleeping and he couldn't believe what he'd just heard. After a terrifying night of cowering from faceless attackers in his dreams, he had to get up and deal with Kylie?

"I hated to have to call and ask for help," Dad said, "but last night was a rough one—I'll feel better if someone's here while I'm at the track."

"It's no problem, Mr. Walsh," Kylie said. "Mary doesn't need my help this morning. She said she'd pick me up after lunch."

Rob could hear Dad showing Kylie around the trailer. He hauled himself into a sitting position on the edge of the bed. He ached. He couldn't tell which hurt worse—his head, his ribs, or his back. He could just glimpse his face in the dresser mirror. "Great," he mumbled as he fell back against the pillow. His lips were puffy and distorted; one eye was swollen shut under the angry, stitched gash; and the other drooped, pulled down by the swelling over his cheekbone. His whole head looked like a bruised and bloodied basketball. Hearing Dad coming down the hall, Rob closed his eyes. He heard his father open the door, pause a moment, and then leave.

"He's still asleep, Kylie," Dad said. "Tell him I'll be back around one."

Dad left and Rob heard Kylie cross the living room. The couch squeaked as she sank onto it. What was he going to do? He didn't want Kylie to see him like this. If he didn't have to go to the bathroom so badly, he'd just pretend to sleep all morning. Rob lay in bed, listening to Kylie flip through the pages of a magazine, the pain in his bladder becoming more insistent by the minute.

His bladder won. When he could stand it no longer, he struggled into his old terrycloth robe and ventured out into the hall. He was too stiff to dash, but he managed to wobble across to the bathroom without, he was fairly sure, Kylie spotting him.

Minutes later, feeling much better, Rob leaned against the sink to study his face in the mirror. Close up, it only looked worse. He knew a soak in a hot tub was what he needed, but he didn't want to be lying around naked with Kylie in the next room. The thought made him smile, though only briefly because of the soreness in his face. Kylie, he knew, was not likely to charge into the bathroom after him.

Rob hobbled from the bathroom to his room and flopped on his bed. He heard Kylie rise from the couch and come toward the bedrooms.

"Rob, are you all right?" she called in her prim voice.

He didn't answer her.

"Rob?" Her voice now sounded soft, concerned.

"Come on back, Kylie," he answered.

But when she entered the room, the look of horror on her face shamed Rob. Girls like Kylie didn't go with guys who got into fights. But then, who was going with Kylie? Not him.

She forced a stiff-lipped smile. "You're a mess," she said.

"I guess I'm not much of a fighter." He looked down at his unbruised hands. "I don't think I even got a punch in."

Kylie looked away. Between them lay an awkward silence, thick and dark like a night fog. Rob could think of nothing to say to remove it.

"Mary said Beak came looking for Dixie and jumped you," Kylie finally said. Rob only nodded. "Rob, Dixie's gone." A cold fear seized his stomach. What did she mean? "The police were at the track this morning to pick up Beak. Your dad must have called early because Mary and I saw them there around seven-thirty. But Beak and Dixie cleared out sometime last night. Both their rooms were empty." Rob sighed, relieved that "gone" meant gone away, not dead. Kylie sat in the chair by the bed. After a few moments, she continued, "Rob, I'm sorry. I know Dixie . . ."

"No, Kylie, you don't understand. I thought when you said 'gone' that Beak had . . . Well, never mind. Kylie, Dixie was just a friend." Kylie looked embarrassed. "Did you think . . . ," Rob began.

"Well, Rob, everybody knows Dixie's reputation, and then that day by the pop machine . . ."

"Kylie, I wasn't screwing Dixie. Jeez, Kylie . . ."

"I'm sure I wasn't the only who thought you were. You were always together, and she hung all over you."

Rob remembered, at one point, hoping Kylie thought he and Dixie had something going. Not now. "If you knew how she got used so badly by everyone, you'd know I just couldn't . . . Kylie, I don't use people."

"Well, she was some friend, running off with Beak after he did this to you," Kylie said, gesturing toward Rob with a fling of her hand, anger evident in her voice.

But Rob didn't feel betrayed by Dixie. Maybe because he'd never expected anything from her—not the usual things expected from a friend, like loyalty and dependability. "I don't think she could help herself, Kylie," he said. He winced, thinking of Beak. "I just hope she's all right."

"You're too easy on her. She didn't have to go with Beak and you know it."

Rob studied Kylie. She was so confident, so sure of who she was and where she was going. She worried that she didn't know exactly what she was going to do with her life, but she still lived each day confident that she was on the right road. Dixie didn't even know there was a road. "Kylie, do you think it's possible that some people might get so lost that finding the way back would take more strength than they have?" Kylie just stared at him. "I mean, some people just don't seem to be very strong."

Kylie looked at him with her brow furrowed. Finally, she said, "I believe people can do whatever they want, Rob." She held herself straight in the chair.

Rob looked away from her. The dark fog again began to rise between them. "Hey, I'm starving," Rob said, dispersing the clouds. "Help me out to the kitchen so I can see what's there."

"That's why I'm here, to get you what you need. You stay in bed and I'll bring you something."

"I'm so sore lying here—I think I might feel better on the couch." Rob dragged himself slowly to his feet, hoping he wouldn't groan in front of her. "Now, if you get my pillows, I'll be able to make it." Rob started toward the door. At the sound of Kylie's laughter, he turned around gingerly. "And what's so damned funny?"

"You. You look like my great-grandfather, who's ninety-three and has arthritis. You're hobbling around like him in that old brown robe with those skinny legs hanging out underneath."

Rob looked down at his legs, bare below the robe, and his short pajama bottoms. He started to laugh and had to hold his ribs. "Don't make me laugh. It hurts too much."

Kylie came up and took his arm. "Maybe I'd better help you."

"We both won't make it through the hall at the same time," Rob answered. But he liked the way her hand felt on his arm. "My legs aren't skinny," he said.

Kylie stepped back and looked at his legs. "They are a little, but remember, I didn't say I didn't like them," she teased.

Rob straightened his back, ignoring the pain as he made his way to the living room. He still had a chance with Kylie. He knew it. He could feel it.

All Kylie was able to find in the nearly bare refrigerator—besides several cans of beer—was a half-filled jar of peanut butter, half a loaf of bread, and some orange juice. Hungry though he was, peanut butter toast and juice was about all Rob could handle. But the last bite of toast with the peanut butter clinging to the roof of his mouth and coating his tongue nauseated him, and he gulped the last of the juice to wash it down. The juice stung his cracked and swollen lips. Rob lay back against the sofa cushions, stretching his legs forward to rest on the coffee table. Too much pressure on his back. He tried to find a comfortable position.

"Can I get you something else? That wasn't much of a breakfast."

"No, I don't think I could get anything else down," Rob answered, giving up on finding a comfortable way to sit and slumping in the corner of the couch.

Neither of them spoke again for a few moments. Rob knew what he had to say to Kylie, but didn't know how to begin. Kylie rose to clear the dishes, and after a few minutes of fidgeting around in the kitchen, returned to the couch. "How about some television?" she asked.

After watching a morning game show and reruns of an ancient sitcom, Rob said, "Kylie, turn that thing off. I have to say something."

Kylie flipped off the television and sat on the opposite end of the couch.

"About that night at the barn," Rob began. "I never should have put the moves on you like that, but I . . . No excuses— I'm really sorry."

Kylie blushed. "That's okay. . . . I mean, it wasn't okay, but I accept your apology."

"Can we go back and try again? I like you, Kylie and . . ."

"Rob, I don't want to get into this," Kylie interrupted. "We're friends, all right?" Rob tried not to look hurt, to look cool. "I'm sorry, Rob. I don't want to hurt your feelings, but you scare me."

"Scare you? For God's sake, Kylie, I'm not a rapist or anything like that."

"But I know you were drunk last night, and that's why Beak was able to do such a job on you. I know you're drunk a lot. I can't figure out if you don't care what happens to you or if you just don't believe anything bad can happen to you. That scares me."

Rob was spared the need to answer by Mary's arrival. They heard her truck pull up in front of the trailer. Kylie jumped up to get the door, then stopped. "Rob, I do like you. I just don't know what I want that to mean," she said.

Mary stayed only long enough to poke around the swellings in Rob's face, check his stitches, and ask how he felt. After accusing her of doing more harm than good with her probing, Rob said good-bye to her and Kylie.

When they were gone, the loneliness that settled on him hurt far worse than his still-stinging face. He wanted to finish that conversation with Kylie. But how could he tell her that lately he'd been scaring himself? He hated going to those parties and he hated not going. The booze numbed the loneliness, but what he felt puking his guts out into one of those foul washroom toilets was worse. And how could he ever explain to anyone the terror of last night? Rob started to sweat; his limbs began to shake. Weakly, he rose to his feet and stumbled across the room to turn on the television—anything to distract him from the fear. As long as someone had been with him, it hadn't come back.

One of television's wackier game shows was on. It would help to keep him occupied until Dad came home. He'd told Kylie one o'clock. It wasn't long until then.

But one o'clock came and went. Damn it. He wanted Dad. Where in the hell was he? But the memory of the night before, with Dad crying helplessly, returned to haunt Rob. He let out a groan from deep in his chest—a long, wailing, painful groan. It was, however, pointless to cry. There was no changing the facts. Dad's being there probably wouldn't help much. Not that Dad wouldn't want to help. Just as he'd intended to be home by one and no doubt felt awful that he hadn't made it. But for whatever reason he chose to give Rob, the truth was that Dad couldn't manage his life well enough to be home by one. He was never where he was supposed to be, and then, when he did arrive . . . It was the same way with Rob's license. Dad did mean to help him get it, but he'd never find the time. Dad, like Dixie, couldn't be depended on. He couldn't help it. It was just the way he was.

But that left Rob all alone again and frightened. Why was this so hard to face about Dad? He'd faced it about Mom long ago. Because now he was utterly alone, with no one to depend on. He had a sudden urge to call Granddad. Rob grabbed the phone next to the couch and dialed Granddad's office number.

After the official company greeting by the secretary, Rob said, "Hi, Judy. It's Rob. Is my granddad in?"

"He sure is, Rob. And I think he's missing you. He just dropped a letter addressed to you into my mail pile. Hold on now."

Almost immediately, Granddad's voice came on the line. "Robbie, how are you doing?"

The tears started to well up in Rob's eyes, urging him to say, "Terrible, Granddad." But instead he said, "Fine. I had a few minutes, so I thought I'd call and say hi."

"Well, I'm glad you did. What's going on down there? Your father hasn't gone off again, has he?"

"No, Granddad. He's here. He's not here in the trailer this minute, but he's not gone away or anything." Rob really didn't have anything to say, unless he was going to tell Granddad what had happened to him.

"Rob, are you sure everything's all right? You don't sound like yourself."

"I'm okay, really." And he was—at least a lot better now that he had someone to talk to, even if he didn't have anything to say. But he couldn't tell Granddad about last night. He'd make him come home now. Home? For the first time, going back to Granddad's didn't seem so bad. But he couldn't go now. Rat had a big race at the end of the week. "Hey, Grand-dad," Rob said, "I want to tell you about this horse I'm taking care of." And Rob told him all about Rat. And Granddad actually seemed interested.

"Rob," interrupted Granddad after a while, "you're not thinking of staying on with the horses and not coming home, are you? I've been suspicious since you left, and now you sound so excited about this horse, and what with your Dad encouraging you . . ."

"Whoa, Granddad. Wait a minute." Rob didn't want Granddad to start in on Dad.

"Say what you're going to say now, Rob. I'd rather we had it all up front." Granddad sounded stern.

Rob took a deep breath. "I was considering it. I love the horses, and I'm good with them. But I don't really know what I want to do."

"I don't like this, Robbie."

"I know you don't."

"Rob, you don't belong there anymore."

"Granddad." He'd been wrong to try to talk to him.

"Listen here, son. I'll keep my mouth shut now. It can wait until you come home. But we'll sit down and have a talk then, won't we? Promise me."

"I promise, but you may not like what I have to say," Rob said, tears welling up in his already-swollen eyes.

Granddad paused before answering. "I only want what's best for you, you know. But maybe we should talk about what you think that is. Not that I won't fight you a bit if I disagree . . ."

Rob blinked back the tears and cleared his throat.

"Rob, you still sound funny to me. What's wrong?"

What could he say? Everything? Nothing? Some jerk beat

the crap out of me last night and might have killed me if he hadn't been stopped? The tears began to sting the corners of his eyes, but he choked them back. "I'm all right, Granddad. Stop worrying." One thing Rob knew for certain—if Granddad knew what had happened, he would be on the next plane into town and Rob would be on the next one back home with him. Rob wasn't ready for that—not yet. Besides, he had to be here for Rat. No one else would be able to hold Rat together, to keep him racing.

"I have to go now. I'll call at the end of the week. Goodbye, Granddad," Rob said, quickly hanging up the phone after Granddad assured him he would be waiting for his call. Rob knew, too, that Granddad would continue to worry. He always did. As long as it didn't prompt him to make any phone calls to the track or to Mary to check on his concerns, Rob didn't mind. Granddad only worried because he loved him. Rob's swollen lips broke into a smile, and it hardly even hurt.

The next day Rob perched stiffly on the tack trunk outside of Rat's stall. Still hurting, he had planned to stay in the trailer for one more day, but by nine o'clock Dad had come for him. Rat refused to let anyone in the stall, not even to feed him.

As they drove up in front of the barn, Rob could hear Rat squealing and kicking the wall of his stall. Under the gaze of the other grooms, Rob managed to stroll—hardly limping— to Rat's stall. "Hey, Rat," he said as he approached the stall. The big horse spun around to face Rob, nickering excitedly and tossing his head. "Rat, I didn't know you cared," Rob muttered as he opened the door. Rob reached to pat the stallion, but he turned his head. "I know, big fella, it's got to be on your terms, doesn't it?"

Dad handed Rat's feed to Rob, who poured it into the feed bucket. Rat immediately dove into his breakfast.

"That's amazing," said Dad when Rob backed out of the stall. "You wouldn't believe what he put us through."

Rob remembered the night of Rat's last race, the night of his beating, when Rat had run him out of the stall. "Yes, I would, Dad. He can be bad." But Rob said it proudly, because after all, as bad as Rat was, he'd just shown Dad and everyone else who it was who could handle him.

Rob enjoyed his new position. Although it was two more days before he could crawl onto the jog cart himself, Rob's presence was necessary to make Rat even moderately tractable. Every day more of the swelling and discoloration left Rob's face and his muscles became less sore. Granddad had not come to take him away. Rat was all right, if not great. It looked as if they were all going to make it for the big race on Saturday night.

On that third day, Rob stood on the gravel drive, holding Rat while Dusty hitched him to the cart. Dad came strutting up the shed row. "You're going to be in the paper, Rob," he said. "There's a reporter here doing a story on the favorites in Saturday's race. It seems that in spite of Rat's antics in his last start, he's still one of the favorites. Anyway, I told him about Rat and how you're the only one who can do anything with him, and he thought it would make a great story."

Rob rubbed Rat's nose. "Did you hear that, boy? We're going to be in the paper." Rat nudged Rob's shoulder. "Come on, Rat. I'm still too sore for much of that."

A photographer took several shots of Rob jogging Rat and even more shots of him caring for the stallion. The article appeared in the morning edition of the local paper on the day of the big race. It was a great story, taking up nearly half a page in the sports section, with a big picture of Rat and Rob. Rob was an instant celebrity with the breakfast crowd in the track cafeteria. He enjoyed their good-natured teasing, calling him "Mr. Celebrity" and "Supergroom."

The article even suggested that with Rob taking care of Rat, he was a likely candidate to win the race. But that night, as Rob led his horse to the paddock, he wasn't so sure. Rat was wild, rearing and balking every few steps. Rob was still too sore from the beating to withstand much wrestling around. "Rat, cut it out," Rob begged as Rat planted his feet and refused to enter the paddock.

"Rob, you need some help?" asked the security guard at the entrance to the paddock.

"Maybe if you just walked around behind him, Mike," Rob said.

"Whatever it takes. You and your horse are our star attractions tonight," Mike laughed.

Somehow they managed to get Rat into the paddock and out onto the track for his first warm-up trip. Rob sat, watching Dad and Rat circle the track. Grooms and drivers, now known to Rob after his weeks at the track, stopped to tease him or to ask how his horse seemed tonight. Rob had emerged from the dark underside of life at the track into the limelight and he liked it. If only he hadn't so impulsively opened up to Granddad about the possibility of his staying on with Dad. But then, the day he'd done it, the beating had still been a terror and his disappointment in Dad fresh and painful. He'd offered it to Granddad as a gift of confidence because then, he thought he'd be going back to Mom and Granddad. Now he wasn't so sure. He liked all of the new attention. He liked knowing he was important to Rat, and he knew Rat was important to him.

"Rob, over here," Kylie called from the path that led to the grandstand. She waved and flashed him the V for victory sign. He crossed his fingers and waved back at her. He sure hoped so. He watched her walk away, all dressed up in her lilac shirtwaist because they were going out after the races. They were all going out for something to eat—Dad and Rob and

Kylie and Mary and Michael and maybe Nicole, too, but that was all right.

As the evening wore on, Rat became more and more restless. Rob began to worry that he might be trampled to death before he had a chance to go out with Kylie. Rat pawed the gravel in front of his paddock stall, and several times Rob thought he struck at him. The stallion tossed his head, his eyes rolling. "Come on, Rat," Rob said. "You're in the next race—it won't be much longer."

"Well, how is he?" Dad asked as he came to help Rob with the final preparations for the race.

"He's really wild, Dad. Watch him." Rat bit at Dad's arm as he tried to adjust the blinders on his race bridle. Dad drew back sharply, and Rat shied as far to the rear of the stall as the cross ties would allow.

"You're not kidding. I've never seen him quite this spooky." Dad eased himself into the stall beside Rat and checked the rest of the harness. "Looks all right to me."

The announcer called the horses for the fifth race. Rob led Rat, with Dad in the sulky, into position. He managed a quick pat on Rat's shoulder and a whispered "Behave yourself, fella" before stepping out of the way to watch the horses parade toward the grandstand. As the horses fell into place behind the starting gate, Rat paced steadily with the others. Uneasiness began to build in Rob. The one thing Rob had always been able to predict about Rat was that he'd toss his head and fuss behind the gate.

Past the paddock they came. Dad seemed to be having trouble holding Rat. He was leaning back on the lines and Rob could see the muscles in Rat's neck and shoulders tense as he pulled against the lines. God, the horse was magnificent. The fiery red of his coat, his size, and his obvious power made him stand out from the rest of the field, which seemed drab in comparison. There was nothing to worry about—Rat looked great.

The starting gate swung open and they were off! Rat surged into the lead in a burst of speed that soon left the rest of the field behind. Rob wanted to laugh. *You show them, Rat.* Three . . . four . . . five lengths Rat put between himself and the field. Rob could hear the murmurs of surprise from the other horsemen in the paddock.

"Look at the timer," someone said.

They had gone the quarter in twenty-eight seconds. The uneasiness returned in a flood. What was Dad thinking of? Rat continued to hold his lead, maybe even gaining another length on the rest of the horses. They went by the half in fifty-seven seconds. The word had gone out. Everyone in the paddock came down to the rail. Only Rob, who caught a glimpse of Dad's face as they went by, knew what was happening.

"That horse must have read this morning's paper," someone laughed.

"Hey, Rob," came another voice. "You tell your horse he was the favorite or something?"

"Looks like Walsh is going for a new record with that red devil of his," someone else said.

No, he's not—Rat's taken off with him, Rob thought. He bit his still-sore lips. With Rat, anything could happen—he was out of control. They were approaching the three-quarter pole. Rob's head began to pound. A silence fell over the crowds in the grandstand and the paddock; they seemed to hold their breath as they waited for what the timer would tell them.

Suddenly Rat hesitated, and then burst into a rolling gallop. A collective moan swept the track. As Dad pulled Rat to the outside and began to saw on the lines, the field gained on them. The attention of the crowd now turned back to the field and to discussion of who would take the lead from Rat. Rob still stared at his horse. Dad was having trouble getting him back on the pace, even though he was sawing forcefully on the lines.

The field raced by Rat and he responded, swinging back onto the pace and charging after them.

"Look. Walsh has his colt back on stride."

But Rob had been watching. Dad hadn't put Rat back on the pace. Rat was still running the race his way. At the back of the pack, a brown pacer made his move. It was Whimsy Pinehill. The other horses were tiring from trying to keep up with Rat. Whimsy Pinehill had been saving himself. "Come on, Rat—don't let him beat you," breathed Rob.

They were now at the top of the grandstand curve. Whimsy Pinehill was pacing on the outside in third place. Rat, also pacing on the outside, had caught the back runners. By the time they had rounded the curve, Whimsy Pinehill had taken the lead and Rat was gaining fast. At the top of the grandstand, Whimsy Pinehill had a length-and-a-half lead as Rat moved into the second slot against the rail.

The finish line was right in front of them. Rat shot again to the outside to pass Whimsy Pinehill. The field surged in behind them. But something was wrong. Rob could feel it. Rat hesitated. This was it. Not even sure what "it" was, Rob screamed, "No!" Rat and Dad crashed to the ground. Rob leapt the paddock fence and began to run toward the grandstand as the field plowed into the fallen horses. The screams from the crowd echoed Rob's own.

Only Whimsy Pinehill and three other horses, one of them without a driver, passed Rob on their way back to the paddock.

The other four horses in the race had fallen over Rat and Dad in a twisted jumble of horses and sulkies and drivers.

Rob reached the accident as officials from the track began to pour through the gate. Security guards fought to keep all others back. Rob couldn't see Dad. At first he couldn't tell which horse was Rat. The horses began to struggle to their feet as did their drivers, holding an arm or rubbing a leg. Only Dad and Rat and one other horse still lay in the dirt.

Rob knelt beside Dad. A man in a suit pushed him out of the way. "Let me in here, boy. I'm a doctor." Numbly, Rob moved aside and watched as the doctor felt for a pulse. "His pulse is strong. You his kid?" Rob nodded. "You can thank the Lord he had on a good helmet and the strap held. That leg's probably broken though." Rob looked at Dad's right leg, twisted under him with a dirt-smudged imprint of a hoof on his thigh. On his other leg blood welled from a slash above the knee to soak his white driving pants. The doctor stood and waved to the ambulance that raced toward them from the opposite end of the grandstand.

Michael and Kylie were beside Rob. Kylie immediately dropped to her knees beside him. Michael went to the doctor. "I'm a friend," he said. "How badly is he hurt?"

The doctor shook his head and shrugged. "I won't know until I get him to the hospital and get some X-rays."

Kylie took Rob's hand and bowed her head as if praying. Impatiently he pulled away from her, looking down the track to where Rat, like Dad, lay unmoving. A group had formed around the other downed horse, pulling the twisted sulky away and untangling lines that had wound around his back legs. Rob recognized Mary at the horse's head, helping the driver pull him to his feet.

The attendants lifted Dad into the ambulance. "If you're going with him," one of them said, "hop in."

"Kylie," Rob said, "please, help Rat."

"Rob, do you want me to come with you?" asked Michael.

Rob crawled into the back of the ambulance next to Dad. He looked past Michael at the motionless body of his horse. Why wasn't Mary helping Rat?

"Rob?" said Michael.

"No, Michael," he said. "Stay and help Rat. Get Mary to help Rat." He looked at Kylie who, though standing, seemed still to be praying. "Kylie?"

The attendants slammed the doors shut, and the ambulance, beacon flashing, raced down the track. Michael and Kylie stared after them.

Rob shook his head and pointed at Rat. No! Michael, Kylie—go help Rat! Get Mary! Make her help Rat!

As the ambulance turned off the track and he could no longer see them, Rob tried to take up the prayer. But words wouldn't come. "Oh . . . please!" he cried as the ambulance sped toward the hospital.

Hours later, a cab dropped Rob back at the barn. Dad had suffered only a concussion and a very clean break of his leg. Dad would be fine. Rob walked slowly toward the barn. The door to Rat's stall hung ominously open. Rob walked out of the barn. He knew where they'd taken him. On through the parking lot, past the administration building, and toward the field behind the final row of barns he walked. His thoughts were formless, numbed by dread and exhaustion.

The night was without stars and the crescent moon had begun to set. Only the vapor lamps shone throughout the complex. Still, when Rob rounded the last row of barns and looked down into the field to where mountains of manure waited to be hauled away, he saw the hulking form of Rat. Dead horses were brought here, too.

Rob fell to his knees beside the body of the big red horse. The way he had fallen, head first, his neck had probably snapped. Rob reached out to stroke Rat's neck, but the cold flesh had begun to stiffen. He pulled his hand away. Dead. Gone. Finished. Rob began to cry. For the first time in years he let the tears flow, no longer wanting to hold them back.

The fiery mane that Rob had so proudly kept free of tangles lay snarled in the dirt. Rob entwined his fingers in the silky red hair. It felt the same as it always had. Rob's tears fell silently until his eyeballs ached. They fell not just for Rat, but for all the sadness that had accumulated since Rob had decided he was too old to cry. He just let the tears come until finally, with a deep sigh and a loud sniff, he squeezed his eyes shut and ordered them to stop. They did, though not immediately. He could control them. Had he been afraid that if he started to cry he wouldn't be able to stop?

Just weeks ago, he hadn't even known this horse. How, then, could his loss hurt so? Rob twisted his hands, buried in Rat's mane, into fists. "You couldn't help yourself. You were just a horse—a dumb old, good old, horse." Shakily, he rose to his feet. He gave Rat one more look.

Rob started back to his room. The many rows of barns nestled in shadows stretched before him—a labyrinth. Almost from the day Dad had first driven him through the gates, he'd gotten lost in it. He had always been sure he could find his way back. But to what?

A truck rounded the last shed row and caught Rob in its headlights. He stiffened.

"Rob?" Mary called. In a moment, Mary and Kylie were at his side, their arms encircling him. He clung to them, accepting the shelter of their warm, firm bodies. He buried his face in Kylie's cool, soft hair. He wasn't ready to let them go when they stepped away from him. But he straightened, feeling the muscles in his back and shoulders pulling him upward.

"Rat's dead," he said, his voice cracking as he forced the words from his throat.

"I know, Rob. He broke his neck when he fell," Mary said.

Rob nodded numbly and looked at Kylie, who had begun to cry.

"Oh, Rob, I'm so sorry," Kylie whispered, slipping her hand into his.

Rob wrapped his fingers through Kylie's and squeezed, unable to speak.

Together they walked to the truck. "We missed you at the hospital, Rob," Mary said. "We couldn't come right away because there were too many horses to be seen. Rat racked up quite a few of them."

Rob's stomach clenched—he felt at least in part responsible. "How bad were they hurt, Mary?"

"They were lucky—nothing too serious. That's the risk of the sport. The drivers are all fine, too. And the hospital tells me that your dad's going to be okay. Come on, I'm taking you back to the trailer, and you're not to worry about getting back here in the morning. Frank and Jan said they'd take care of your horses."

They rode silently toward the trailer park, with Kylie holding tightly to his hand. Mary's words had comforted him a little. Still, he and Dad had known how dangerous Rat could be. "It's just that we had such dreams for him," he said aloud.

"That's the thing about horses—they can't dream for themselves. They don't even plan, at least not what we'd call planning. They react. Most react in ways we can predict. Rat never did. He'd had enough and he reacted. I'm sure he didn't think about the consequences."

As the truck rolled on toward the trailer court, Rob slipped his arm around Kylie, who snuggled into his shoulder. He wanted her to know he cared and wanted to be near her, with no greater expectation than closeness. He breathed in the light floral smell of her perfume mixed with the smell of antiseptic and liniment. He liked how she smelled.

Rob looked at Mary's profile against the window. Though her hair was pulled into its usual braid, wispy tendrils had pulled free in the heat and exertion of the evening to circle her head. Her short-fingered, capable hands rested lightly on the wheel.

Mary turned the truck into the trailer court and drove by Tillie and Ernie's trailer. For the first time in weeks, Rob didn't turn his head away, but no fuzzy pink head popped from the darkened window and no bent, gray-haired form slouched on the patio. It was still night, only creeping toward dawn. Tomorrow morning he'd go to see them. They were sure to have heard about the accident and would want to know the details.

When Mary pulled up to his trailer, first Kylie and then Rob stepped out of the truck. "Mary, thanks . . . for everything," he said.

"Are you going to be all right?" Mary asked.

Rob swallowed hard. He heard the huskiness in his voice as he spoke. "I'll be fine, Mary. I need some sleep. There's an awful lot I'll have to do tomorrow. Rat's owner wasn't at the races tonight. I'll have to call him. I've got to call Mom and Granddad and see if I can stay a while longer. Dad's going to need help."

"I thought you'd decided to stay and become your dad's partner," Mary said.

"I don't know, Mary. When I'm driving a horse, I feel so good, so sure of myself. But I promised Granddad I'd talk to him before I made a decision. I guess I still have a lot to think over."

Kylie reached under the seat and pulled out a package wrapped in white tissue paper and decorated with a red bow.

"Michael and I want you to have this. We were going to give it to you after the races tonight. Now I want you to have it more than ever." Kylie started to get back into the truck.

"Aren't you going to wait for me to open it?" he asked.

"No," Kylie said, smiling with tears in her eyes. She hugged him quickly before climbing back into the truck.

"You're sure you're all right?" Mary asked.

"I'm sure," he answered, forcing a smile.

When they drove off, Rob went into the trailer, cradling the tissue-covered box. He had a pretty good idea of what was inside and was glad he was alone to open it.

Sitting on the couch, he removed the ribbon, paper, and cardboard box top. Inside, he parted more tissue to reveal what he had known would be there—Michael's carving of Rat. It hadn't been complete when Rob last saw it. Michael had not yet carved the delicate legs that now stretched out in a free-legged pace. A thin wire held the carving poised above the base, so that the horse seemed to be flying. The deep, natural red of the wood was so much like Rat's coat. Rob ran his index finger over the polished wood. He was going to miss Rat, but he didn't need the carving to remind him of his horse. Rat was unforgettable. The carving would serve him better as a reminder of friends.

He sat studying the carving, thinking about Rat, about all that had happened since he'd come back to Farmington. A horn sounded far off on the main road, making Rob realize how silent the trailer park was at night. Usually he hated the lonely quiet of nighttime. That was when his heart drummed in his chest, his limbs shook, his breath came in shallow gasps, he poured sweat. But tonight he didn't mind being alone. Maybe because he knew he didn't have to be. He could have gone home with Mary and Kylie. And he knew he could call

Granddad, and, even though the call would wake him, Grand-dad wouldn't mind. But Rob could wait until morning.

He carried the carving to his bedroom and placed it in the center of the dresser before preparing for bed. He stripped down to his underwear and climbed between the sheets, but sleep wouldn't come. As Rob lay there, his mind seemed to swirl deep into a labyrinth and then out again to soar above, where all the paths, the choices, were clear. He saw a lot of people who were lost in that maze: Dusty . . . Dixie . . . Beak . . . Dad . . . even Mom. Many paths led in descending circles deeper into the labyrinth, but there were just as many leading out into the open. When he looked more carefully he saw that from many of the paths that led out friendly hands beckoned, but few of the people moving through the maze seemed to stop long enough to notice them. But where was he? Rob knew he was still there. Which path should he take? Steely bands of fear began to squeeze Rob's chest. He jumped to his feet, snapping himself back from his dream.

He walked to his window, which faced the eastern sky. As he watched, the first ray of light spread over the horizon—pink, then orange, then yellow. "Oh, God, it's beautiful," he breathed. He watched the sunrise swell. Daylight was coming. He'd find his way now.

Rob slipped on his jeans and, barefooted, stepped onto the porch to watch the light blossom. Any day that began with such promise was worth going out to meet.

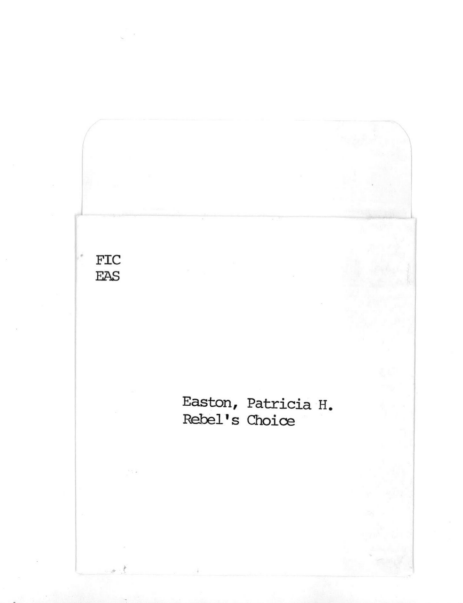

Easton, Patricia H.
Rebel's Choice